Ouji
The Curious Cat

By Blair Cousins

To: Jay

Blair

For contact information - www.facebook.com/BlairCousinsAuthorPage/

Cover design by Streetlight Graphics, LLC

Dedication design by Charlotte Hartle

ISBN: 978-0-9984621-0-3

First Edition - 2017

10 9 8 7 6 5 4 3 2 1

This book is dedicated to the little girl who dared to dream and
dared to take that next step forward.

Special thanks to FF, my friends, and family
for their supportive words

Chapter one

The mid-day sun shined through the blinds of Ouji's home, casting parallel lines on the floor. Adrian, Ouji's newest friend, made himself comfortable on the arm of the couch, watching Ouji with a soft smile on his face. Adrian twitched his long gray whiskers, before settling in and watched his new friend stare curiously off into the distance. "Why don't you tell me about your life?"

Ouji turned. "My life?" Ouji tilted his head, as he had never been asked about his life before. There was nothing interesting as far as Ouji could tell, but the look on Adrian's face invited Ouji to open up. "Well, I'm not sure where to begin."

The tiny black kitten opened his eyes for the very first time. The world around him was bright and unfamiliar, his senses overloaded with the many sights and smells. He stumbled, tripping over his paws and the tiny folds in the sea of blankets, surrounded by huge metal walls. He looked up at the steel sky, mesmerized by its vastness. He meowed softly and rolled over onto his back feeling content to lay there for as long as this existence lasted.

Suddenly there was a sound and a gentle vibration in the blankets. He lifted his tiny head, and his dark brown eyes darted around. He rolled onto to his stomach as his little ears perked atop his head. He lifted his nose and caught the sweet familiar aroma of his mother. Gentle wafts of her scent floated in the air, surrounding him like a blanket. He closed his eyes and sought comfort in it, nuzzling deeper into the blankets that too smelled like her. When she approached she purred affectionately. Ouji opened his eyes and marveled at the deep brown eyes staring back at him.

A passing car caused Ouji to blink and looked around the room, torn from his dream. Those old memories flooded his mind and even though he hadn't seen his mother in years it felt like only yesterday that she was right there beside him. His memories of her were his most treasured possession. The tiny mouse watched as the black cat reveled in his memories as if he had forgotten the mouse was there at all. Adrian understood the familiar expressions on his face, as he too hadn't seen his family in a very long time. He wrinkled his nose and encouraged Ouji to continue. Ouji smiled and nodded and immersed himself once more in his memories.

Life in the big metal box was full of adventure for the tiny kitten and his siblings. Every day like clockwork, giants, who mother called humans, would bring fresh food and water for their mother. Ouji and his siblings, however were never interested in the stinky stuff their mother ate and kept busy by playing with all the fascinating objects all around them. There were bright shiny balls that jingled and soft plush mice and rope tied to the gates of their home. It was paradise to the kittens and when lunch came they would fill themselves up on their mother's sweet milk and nap the rest of the day away. To Ouji his mother was the most beautiful creature he had ever seen. He loved her glowing orange and white fur that striped down her sides and disappeared under her belly. Her fur was softer than anything he'd ever touched and so very warm too. During the cold nights he'd bury himself next to his siblings deep down in her soft fur. There was no better feeling than sleeping next to her and his siblings.

At night he felt safe to dream, drawing comfort his mother's deep throaty purrs, like lullabies that carried him off to sleep. By day he would return the gesture, trying to replicate her purrs. The noises that came from his throat sounded different, and it felt even stranger as the jagged hum vibrated his entire body. It fascinated him as he showered his mother with purrs that were met with eyes full of love and affection.

Ouji's siblings were his best friends, though they didn't look like him. Ark, his brother, was a brown and black tabby; stripes covered his entire body. His sister Sun was all white except for a few spots of orange on her eyes, ears, and the tip of her tail. She was also the bravest of the three, always eager to play and explore. She was quick on her paws and even though Ouji could never keep up that didn't stop him from trying. He chased her around their steel home, under the blankets and into the litter pan, and right over their mother. Their games of tag were like mini complex obstacle courses. His brother Ark, who was a bit smaller than them, watched from the safety of the bed, where he would hide and jump out and tackle whoever veered too close. The humans always fussed over him. Ouji never understood why; Ark ate the most and played the hardest despite his size. Ouji once saw Ark climb to the top where the cage bars met the steel sky. He marveled at the feat though when he tried his mother was quick to pull him down by his scruff.

Finally a day came Ouji thought never would. One day the humans came and took his mother away. At first he and his siblings thought she would be right back as she had been time and time again, so they waited. They waited all day even after the humans brought their dinner. They waited. Humans came and went, but never once did they come back with their mother and it was the last time Ouji ever saw her.

Ouji blinked himself back to reality, the memories too sad for him to continue. He frowned as his tail flicked lazily from side to side. He didn't want to dwell on these sad thoughts any more. Suddenly there was a sound at the front door. The humans were home. Ouji panicked, jumping into action. He looked at Adrian and without saying a word the little mouse nodded and headed back to the crack from which he came.

"Wait, Adrian!" Ouji peeked behind the kitchen cupboards, before the tiny mouse disappeared. "Will I ever see you again?"

"If you promise not to eat me." Adrian joked.

"Yes of course. I... I would like to know more about the outside world." Ouji stole desperate looks between the mouse and the kitchen door.

Adrian nodded. "I must go now. I will see you again tomorrow when the sun is at its highest point."

"Thank you!" he shouted as his new friend disappeared into the darkness.

The door unlocked and the humans came in. "Martha!" The tall hairy human shouted to the longed haired human. "The cat is on the counter again!" Ouji didn't care for the heavy footed one. He always shouted and stomped around like the roaring sky. Ouji jumped from the counter quickly to avoid his wrath. The long-haired human, Martha shooed Ouji. "Paul, you know better." Martha would always point to him and call him Paul. Ouji thought this might have been his name, but he had been known to humans by many names: Kitten,

Jose, Cat, Furball, and this was latest on the list. By now he just played along with it; he came when the humans called so he could receive his back rubs and head scratches. After all, humans didn't speak cat. They were the only creatures Ouji could not understand, not that he had very many conversations with other animals, he could understand the ones on the flashing box.

Ouji made a beeline for the kitchen table as the big burly human stomped around talking to Martha. The smallest human in the house was a little girl named Samantha. Ouji liked her a lot. She was always nice and spoke to him in a soft voice. He loved to stare into her big blue eyes that always seemed to glow when he was around. He enjoyed her soft strokes as she was the only one to hit the spot just right every time. Every night he would sleep next to her in her large cozy bed. Ouji found a spot next to her on the couch as she pulled out some papers from her knapsack. He watched her pencil write down shapes and lines as she did everyday when she returned home. Samantha was the one who pointed him out at the shelter, some three years ago. She looked at him like they were long lost friends, and though he was sure he had never met her before, he felt safer around her.

That night on her bed Ouji thought about the events that took place before. He made a new friend today, someone from the outside. Ouji purred contently, chuckling to himself at their humorous first encounter. Adrian was filled with such fright, for reasons Ouji could never understand, but after a great deal of explaining Ouji convinced Adrian that he wasn't going to harm him. In fact Ouji was overjoyed at the opportunity to meet and talk to someone new. Ouji sat up and yawned as he stared out the window. All the memories from before made him ponder his own existence. For as long as Ouji could remember his entire life had been an ambiguous black hole of seamlessly unrelated events. He felt like a passenger in his life. With no one to talk to how could he be certain that what he was experiencing wasn't any different than what any other cat was experiencing? It seemed normal to everyone around him so it must be true; however he couldn't shake the feeling that there was more to life beyond the painted walls of his home.

The morning came and the humans scurried around the house quickly gathering their things. Ouji never understood why they were in such a big hurry, so he quietly watched them making sure to stay out of their way. Martha, the long-haired human, prepared food in the kitchen, which always smelled better than the cat food they fed him. In haste she grabbed his food from the cupboard and cracked it open. She scooped it into his blue bowl and added water, mixing it up before placing it on the floor. Ouji watched from the comfort of the den, uninterested in the wet mush waiting for him on the kitchen floor. The loudest human, who they called Scott, opened the closet door and grabbed his jacket from the hanger. He always seemed to be in the biggest rush. Once Ouji made the mistake of blocking his path and nearly caused him to trip. The man hissed and cursed under his breath, but Ouji didn't stick around to try to make things better. To

Ouji Scott always seemed to be in a foul mood, so he kept his distance. Ouji stretched and purred when he saw Samantha running down the stairs. He hopped down from the couch and rubbed his head on her long slender legs. She returned his kindness with a gentle scratch right behind the ears. Her mother called for her and just like that all three of his housemates were gone. He watched them pull off in their metal machine and disappear into the distance, wondering eagerly when they would return or where they were going.

Ouji spent the rest of the morning staring out the window. He watched the sun crawl across the sky waiting patiently for it reach its highest point. He wondered where Adrian slept at night or if he had a home. He wondered if the little mouse had humans as well or did he live outside like the other animals. He thought about this long and hard until his thoughts were interrupted by the sound of his growling stomach. He leaped from the window sill and walked into the kitchen towards his food bowl. He only received the canned food on certain days, but it was no better or worse than the hard food which he normally got. After breakfast he groomed himself, licking his long black fur with his comb like tongue. He took his time starting at the tip of his tail and working his way up as far as he could reach before finishing the rest with his paws.

When he was done he stretched and took to wandering around the house. It was so big when he first moved in, filled with so many different rooms and hiding places, but now it seemed like it was getting smaller and smaller the more he grew. He shook his head, chasing away those thoughts, and stuck to his daily exploring. He started in the master bedroom where the two biggest humans slept and made his way to the master bathroom. He liked to poke around on the toilet seat and play with the tiny trinkets they kept on there. He loved to pick out the tiny black hair ties and little boxes of soaps the humans placed in the basket. To Ouji these were no ordinary objects, they were perfect treasures made to be taken and hidden. Once he was done hiding his treasures he headed towards Samantha's room. He liked it in there because it was soft and smelled like the stuff Martha sprayed on the couch downstairs sometimes. He leaped onto the bed and kneaded the perfectly tucked in sheets, but just as he about to settle in for a nap he remembered that he had a very important appointment today. He rushed towards to the window, feeling a sense of relief as the sun was not yet in position. He leaped down from the window and decided to play with some of the toys that Samantha had on the floor. She always left her tiny dolls and stuffed animals on the floor and when Ouji was younger he thought her toys were the bodies of real animals. He laughed at the thought now, feeling silly that he ever thought such a thing.

Ouji left her room and headed downstairs to another one of his favorite rooms the place where the humans hung their wet clothes. There was always something interesting in there. Hanging from the ceiling would be a forest of drying towels, pants, and blouses. Sometimes there would be sneakers that would go into the rumbling machine very smelly and come out smelling of perfume. Ouji however preferred hanging pants. He looked around for a pair and found some hanging from the rack. He extended his claws and stretched as he dug his nails into the damp fabric. He smiled contently to himself as he made tiny holes in the drying pants, rubbing his body of the legs of the garment. Nothing was better than hanging pants, Ouji was convinced. He walked back to the window in the den to watch the sky; the sun had not moved much so he watched the clouds go by instead. With a sigh, the idea of taking a quick nap sounded more and more appealing. So he made himself comfortable on the kitchen table. At least he would be in the right room, so he could meet Adrian when he came.

"Mr. Ouji?" the little mouse tilted his head. "Mr. Ouji?"

Ouji opened his eyes and saw his new friend hovering just inches over his black nose. "Adrian," Ouji purred as he shut his eyes and flexed his long sharp claws.

"I have returned as promised," Adrian swallowed nervously at the sight of Ouji's long white claws.

"It's so good to see you again." Ouji smiled fondly as he shook the rest of the sleep from his eyes.

"Shall we begin? I am interested to hear more about your life." Adrian said as he plucked a ripe grape from the fruit basket on the table. "What happened after the humans took your mother away?" The little mouse said eagerly.

"Well let's see," Ouji tilted his head and stared off into the distance.

Ouji and his siblings eventually got over the loss of their mother as the weeks turned to months. Though her memory never faded they knew now more than ever that they needed to stick together. So they ate the food the humans left for them and played with each other every day which made the feelings of loneliness fade away.

On a particularly uneventful day the humans came in with a box. In it the siblings could hear a familiar meow. They all ran to the front of the cage to see who it was. The humans opened the box as their little eyes got wider, but the cat they pulled from the box was not their mother. It was a large brown tabby with long fur and black stripes. The little kittens watched as the humans wrestled the cat out of the box and tossed him into the cage above them. The tiny kittens watched and poked their little heads through the bars and listened. Ouji and Ark wouldn't dare say a word but Sun wanted to know more about the other cat above them. After all this would be the first cat they had ever met. Sun lifted herself up, placing her tiny paws on the silver cage bars so that she was now standing on her back legs. She cried out a tiny hello, but Ouji quickly hushed her. He wasn't sure what that other cat would do to them if they spoke, but Sun wasn't afraid. So she called out to the other cat again.

From the top cage came a low raspy growl like rolls of thunder from the sky, followed by a long terrifying hiss. It was nothing like the soft purrs of their mother and it scared Ouji and Ark to their core. Sun gulped and looked back at her brothers, but it was clear from their expressions that she was on her own. Sun stepped forward and looked up in the direction she heard the noise come from. She cleared her tiny throat and asked where the cat had come from. The larger cat growled deeply, brushing off their comments. It was clear that the other cat wanted nothing to do with them. The little kittens frowned, huddling together in their bed in the back of their cage, as they settled in for the night.

As the days went by they realized the humans would bring in different cats from time to time. Sometimes they would bring in other kittens or other cats. This gave the little kittens hope their mother would return but she never did, but that didn't stop Ouji from watching the door every day. Slowly his yearning for his mother turned into curiosity for the outside world. He wondered who the humans were and where they went each day. He wanted to see and explore their world, which he was sure was a lot bigger than the tiny cage he lived in. At night Ouji would listen to the stories of the other cats about the places they had come from. He and his siblings were captivated by the things they heard, about rows of large painted houses and black streets filled with racing metal monsters. These things were too wild and exotic to believe, but the kittens were eager to hear about them. As the kittens grew bigger they outgrew their tiny metal cage. Ouji and Sun were the biggest and most plump of the three, but Ark didn't seem to grow at all. They became worried when he stopped eating and drinking, it was as if something was sucking all his energy away. Sun groomed his nose, licking off the crust that formed there. With no one to guide them, they were not sure what to do to.

Later that day, just a few minutes before dinner the humans opened the cage and checked each kitten as they did from time to time. They lingered over Ark, talking amongst themselves and when they were done they nodded to each other and left the room. Sun watched the human's faces; something was not right she could feel it. She rushed over to Ark and urged him to eat and play. Ouji paid no mind to the humans and their strange ways. He was too concerned with playing with the hanging ball of string tied to the cage.

The humans returned later and opened their cage as they did many times before. Two humans spoke with each other and one opened a brown box they had brought with them and started picking up each kitten, starting with Sun. She meowed loudly as she was scruffed and placed into a box. This caught both Ark and Ouji's attention. Ark was too weak to fight back and Ouji watched in terror as his siblings were taken away from him. He ran to the back of the cage as the human reached inside to grab him. He was scruffed and placed into the brown box with his siblings. The humans closed it up. The kittens were surrounded by darkness with the only light coming from the tiny holes at the top of above them. The ground started to move and the kittens wobbled and fell on top of each other, their tiny paws slipping on the smooth cardboard. They heard the door open and meowed loudly in fear.

The only thing running through Ouji's mind was where they were going. He thought of his mother as the humans carried them away. He wobbled back and forth and looked out of one of the tiny holes of the box. He saw the other side of the door. He fell backward onto Ark who meowed and jumped into Sun, but Ouji didn't notice; he was too busy looking outside at the changing world around him. He watched as his world faded into the distance. As quickly as his journey started it ended when the kittens heard the humans open another door. The box shook and turned and landed on the ground with a thud. The kittens huddled together when the humans opened the box. They could hear the sounds of cats meowing all around them; there must have been over twenty cats in this room and that frightened the little ones. One of the humans reached down and picked up Ark first and placed him into a cage on the top and closed the door. Ouji and Sun bolted for the edge of the box, hiding in the corner. Sun was scruffed at once and placed into a cage. Ouji clawed his way up the cardboard box and was nearly over the top when the humans scooped him up and placed him in the same cage with Sun. The humans closed the door, leaving them separated. Sun looked around for her missing brother. The cage was much smaller than the one they had just left. It smelled of cleaning spray and fresh laundry. There was a metal shelf wedged in the half way point between the top and bottom of the cage with a bowl on the shelf and a litter pan on the bottom. She looked in the rectangular litter box and over the shelf, but she could not find her brother. Sun ran to the cage bars and cried for him. She cried until she heard a tiny little meow from above. He wasn't far, just a cage above them to the left. The kittens meowed in relief as each of them were accounted for. Ouji was terrified. He called for his mother, in hopes she had been taken here too, but he could not distinguish her voice from all the cats meowing around him.

Ouji meowed and meowed, as he climbed to the top of the cage bars and fell over into the bed of sheets. He rolled over to his tummy in defeat when he heard a distant purr. He tilted his head and listened again it softly floated into his ears. He hushed Sun and she watched as her brother honed in onto the hidden sound. Next to them they could hear the deep purrs of the cat beside them. They sounded just like their mother's, deep and full of love and affection. Ouji and Sun walked to the edge of the cage to see who this mysterious cat was.

Her name was Bertha, when she finally spoke in her deep soothing voice. She had been living in this room for long enough to know every cat that lived there. She told the little kittens not to be afraid and that their time here would short. The kittens were relieved to hear this. Ouji poked his tiny head through the metal bars to get a look at Bertha next door. He couldn't see her fully but he saw her long legs sticking through the cage bars. She was a brown and black striped tabby just like Ark, but she was much bigger even then their mother. Ouji watched as she yawned and stretched her enormous arms, unsheathing her long white claws. "Do not be afraid, little ones," she told them, as she relaxed her legs and kneaded the air.

Ouji asked if she had seen their mother, but Bertha told them no. She told them she had been in places like these many times before and that the humans were very nice here. She told them of a time that would come soon when they would leave this place and move into homes. The kittens were amazed and she told them not to worry about their brother Ark, for the humans would care for him too. When night fell Ouji and Sun huddled together in the quiet room. Ouji thought of his brother and how cold he must be. He worried about him and wished he could be by his side, but the calming purrs of their new friend Bertha helped them fall asleep on their first night in the new room.

Adrian lowered his ears. "Was that the last time you saw your brother?" Ouji nodded. It pained him that this was such a common story. "I'm sorry Ouji."

"It's okay," Ouji mustered up a smile.

Adrian smiled back, when he realized how late it was he jumped. "Oh my! I must get going."

"So soon?" Ouji frowned.

"Yes, but I promise to come again tomorrow." The old mouse scurried off.

Ouji watched him leave through the hole in the cupboard. He had not thought of his brother in such a long time. He missed him dearly and wondered often where he had ended up.

When the humans returned he was lying on his cat bed in the den. He didn't feel like greeting anyone and watched the humans walk. He closed his eyes contently as Samantha patted him behind the ears.

When night fell Ouji left his spot beside Samantha and headed downstairs to look out the window. The sky was clear but there was a chill in the air. The window fogged when he breathed on it. It was quiet; most of the homes had their lights turned off. Ouji looked up at the sky. He watched the stars flicker in the sky around the moon. He thought about all the stories he had heard as a kitten and wondered if any of it was true. He looked down the street, past the stop sign, and houses in the distance. In the darkness he wondered if there were places without humans, without homes. A place where the water ran free between the trees and cats didn't live in cages or homes. He watched a lone car pass. Where did the humans go when they left every morning, and why was he trapped in the house while other animals roamed free? In the night sky he watched a flock of birds fly pass and settled in the window sill for the night.

Chapter Two

Ouji sat on the couch watching Adrian eat from a bag of crackers the humans left out on the table. The mouse ate as if he hadn't eaten in a while which made Ouji wondered how food was gathered outside the glass sliding doors.

"Adrian?" Ouji asked, as the little gray mouse turned and looked at him. "What's the outside world like?" Ouji asked curiously.

Adrian perked up his large round ears and looked fondly out the big glass sliding doors in the kitchen. "Oh it's lovely, it's cold in the winters and warm in the spring. The grass grows a marvelous shade of green in the summer and in the fall the ground is covered in red, yellow, and brown leaves. It's tough, but I'd rather be..." Adrian stopped himself; he didn't want to confuse the house cat. He cleared his throat and licked and groomed his face. "Let me start from the beginning. Do you know where you are Ouji?"

Ouji's pupils restricted, exposing the irises of his big brown eyes. He tilted his head. "I'm where the humans live."

Adrian smiled warmly. "The place where you live is called a home, Ouji. Humans make them to live in. When humans make a lot of homes, it is called a neighborhood. These 'neighborhoods' are large communities where they raise their young."

Ouji eyes brightened. He was excited to learn more. "And beyond that?"

Adrian stared at the ceiling and thought. "Beyond that are long stretches of black tar called roads and then there are cities where humans go by day. Cities are far more dangerous though. I wouldn't recommend them."

"And beyond that?" Ouji was on the edge of his seat with excitement. Suddenly his world was opening up. He now knew about neighborhoods and cities, confirming the stories he had heard as a kitten.

Adrian thought for a minute. "I suppose beyond that is the forest."

Ouji tilted his head to the other side. "For-est? What is a forest?"

"The most beautiful and peaceful place you could ever imagine. There are trees as tall as houses that bloom across the sky. There are hundreds of them stretching for miles, with streams as clear as rain that grow into powerful rivers. The air is clean and smells of fresh wood and earth and is quiet and peaceful. I miss it there, I made my journey from the forest to the neighborhoods ages ago. I guess you can say I'm somewhat of an adventurous mouse." Adrian chuckled, but he had to stop himself. He was very familiar with the look in Ouji's eyes. "But the forest is no place for a house cat."

Ouji drooped his ears. The forest sounded like a nice place as his mind tried to formulate an area that vast.

"You belong here Ouji; the humans take very good care of you and feed you and offer you shelter." Adrian took another bite of his butter cracker. He didn't want to sound harsh, but the outside world was filled with as much danger as there was beauty.

Ouji turned over to his side in disappointment. "So you would say living in a home is normal?" he asked.

Adrian nodded, his crooked whiskers bouncing up and down. "Of course. There are outside and inside cats, but you're an inside cat and there is nothing wrong with that." He mentally kicked himself for mentioning outside cats.

"Outside cats?" Ouji looked up, raising his head from the table.

"Yes, they live outside." Adrian didn't want to give Ouji any sense of false hope, the outside world was no place for a house cat.

Ouji stood on all fours. "Really! I'd love to meet them, would you introduce me?"

Adrian shook his head, waving his paws at the black cat. "Oh no, I couldn't. The outside world is no place for an indoor cat."

"Oh please, oh please!" Ouji begged.

Adrian knew that look in Ouji's eyes and he supposed it was too late now to convince Ouji otherwise. Adrian sighed. What a can of worms he had opened. "If I do, you must promise me you'll stay out of trouble. It's a different world out there and if you leave, your humans may not want you back again." Adrian warned.

It was the first time someone offered Ouji a choice. He was so excited he could feel his heart beating right out of his chest. Only in his wildest dreams did he imagine that he would get to go outside. The idea was frightening and wonderful to him.

"Adrian." Ouji bent down right to Adrian's eye level. "Please help me go out into the outside world."

Adrian worried for his new friend, but it was the least he could do in exchange for all the kindness Ouji had shown him. "If you insist, but it will take me a few days to find the right cats. Those outside cats can be a real pain." The gray mouse shook his head. "Give me three days, but I warn you, what lies beyond those big glass doors is a world filled with danger."

Adrian's warning fell on deaf ears as Ouji was too excited about the idea of leaving his home to care. He wished he could have talked to Adrian for longer, but their time was up. The humans would be home any minute. Ouji said his goodbyes to his friend and watched him leave through the tiny hole in the cupboard. It didn't bother him at all when the humans came home, because in three days he would be in the outside world and he couldn't wait.

Night fell and Ouji crawled up next to Samantha in her soft comfy bed. He kneaded and curled beside her as his mind filled with sleep. He wished so very much that the time would fly by and yawned and fell asleep.

"Will you promise me something?" his sister Sun whispered to him in the dead of the night. "Will you promise me that you will never leave me?"

Ouji cuddled next to her. "I promise." Ouji said, half asleep.

Ouji curled up next to his sister in the middle of their soft bed made of sheets. The lights flicked on and Ouji awoke. A minute had hardly passed. The humans came in with another brown box and the two fled to the back of their cage. The humans opened the cage, reached in, and scruffed Sun.

"Help! Help!" Sun screamed.

Ouji was immediately on his paws. He hissed and pounced on the humans, but his tiny paws were no match for their giant heads. The humans placed Sun in a brown box and reached in to put Ouji into another one. Both sat in separate boxes next to each other as they heard the humans stump around.

"I'm scared." Sun whimpered.

"It's okay." Ouji meowed. "Don't be afraid." Ouji tried to be brave. "I'll get us out of here."

Ouji didn't have a clue how to save Sun or himself, but that didn't stop him from trying. He was pulled out of his train of thought by the sudden movement of the box. He could hear the humans above him. The door opened and the two were carried away into another room. Ouji stuck his nose through the tiny holes outside the box trying to sniff out his sister, but all he could smell was the heavy scent of rubbing alcohol and latex. The box opened and Ouji was placed into a cage filled with newspaper. He could see the humans opening Sun's box and he called to her. She saw Ouji and meowed back. Two other humans gathered and checked her, lifting her legs and tail, like they were going to dismantle her. He meowed to her; he could sense the fear in her voice. He clawed against the cage bars trying to reach her as one human scruffed her and held out her leg and laid her on her side. He watched as another human withdrew from his pocket a syringe with a long sharp pointy needle. They pressed it into Sun's back leg. Ouji turned away. She screamed and Ouji jumped on the cage bars in rage. She called to him until her eyes closed.

"Sun!" Ouji screamed as he woke from his nightmare, in a fit.

He woke Samantha by mistake and the little girl turned over and grunted. "Hush Paul, I'm tryin'na sleep." The little girl turned over, pulling the covers over her shoulder.

Ouji tried to settle down, but the nightmare chased away any sleep left in him. He stayed with Samantha until she fell asleep again and looked out the window. The wind caused the shadows of the trees to swing back and forth on the walls of her room. He whispered his sister's name under his breath as he remembered the first night he ever spent alone. When sleep finally caught up with him he dreamed of a world where no one was lonely, a world with no cages or homes, and a world where he and his family could live together forever.

Morning came as it always did. Even with the nightmares from the night before, Ouji looked forward to Adrian's return. In only two days he would be free and be able to explore the world around him like he always wanted to. He stared at the backyard and watched squirrels chase each other around the yard. Their playful chase reminded him of a friend he made when he was little. It was his very first memory of speaking to another animal that was not a cat.

Ouji was crying alone in his metal cage lined with newspaper when he heard a high pitched voice pierce the silence of the night.

"Whatcha cryin' for?" The voice asked.

Ouji didn't reply at first. He was becoming used to drowning out the noises of the shelter and he was not in the mood to entertain whoever was trying to talk to him.

"It's okay, I won't bite. My name's Checker, what's yours?" Checker asked in a softer but no less enthusiastic voice.

Ouji huffed in annoyance and looked away from where he heard the voice. He wanted nothing but to be left alone which was quite the opposite of his true desire. Finally after many long minutes he finally responded to Checker.

"My name is Furt." Ouji meowed softly.

"Furt? What kind of name is that?" Checker asked.

Ouji huffed. "It's my name, the one my momma gave me!"

"That's weird!" Checker laughed.

Ouji could hear the cat's tail slapping against the metal cage. He wondered what kind of cat could be so noisy. "No it's not! Besides you're weird, you're the nosiest cat I've ever met!" Ouji snapped.

Ouji thought he heard Checker laugh again. He lifted his head to see what was so funny. In the darkness it was hard to see, but he could diffidently smell him. His musty breath burned the hairs in his nose and the smell of his fur was sour. Nothing like any cat he'd ever smelt before.

"I'm not a cat silly! I'm a dog!" Checker barked, his voice raised a pitch with his excitement.

Ouji perked up his ears. "A dog? What's a dog?"

"I'm a dog!" Checker barked again.

Ouji rolled his eyes. "I know, but what is it?"

There was a long pause before Checker responded. "Well, a dog is, a dog! You know, we jump and lick a lot. Oh and chase balls and wag our tails!"

"Cats don't wag their tails." Ouji turned up his nose. "Besides why are you being so friendly? There's nothing to be happy about."

"Sure there is! There's yummy food, new dogs-I mean cats to meet, and the humans always give the best belly rubs."

"Yeah, right before they take you away and leave you alone." Ouji retorted.

"You're not alone!" Checker barked "You've got me! And we have each other!"

Ouji looked into the darkness. It never occurred to him that Checker might have had his family taken away from him too. He thought he was all alone, but all the animals here were stuck, trapped behind silver metal bars waiting, waiting for their chance at freedom. Ouji meowed a soft thank you to his new friend.

"Hey cat! You can't go around with a name like that! How about I give you a new one?"

Ouji got up and walked over to the cage bars, he never gave his name much thought. "You'd do that for me?"

"Sure!" Checker barked. "How about I call you Ouji!"

"O-u-ji?" Ouji tilted his head.

"Yeah! You like it? It's what my mom always used to say. Ouji Dah Tiji it means always be with you!" Checker barked, lifting his paws onto the cage bars.

"Ouji Dah Tiji, thank you!" Ouji smiled hard as his heart began to warm again.

He was so grateful for Checker's kindness and he kept his name, his precious gift from his first friend. It reminded him that as long as he held onto the memory of his friends and family he would never be alone.

The humans arrived home at their usual time. Martha prepared supper in the kitchen, while Scott and Samantha watched TV in the den. Ouji was feeling rather happy today, a feeling he only got when the humans opened up the cans of orange cat food in the winter. He walked around the house, taking a seat on the floor by the kitchen door. Adrian said humans live in homes where they raised their young. He wondered how they came to live with cats. He didn't want to think of himself as merely just another object in the home, because when he was around Samantha he really did feel like he was apart of the family. He would miss her, but it was time for him to move on. His life here was becoming stale, and each day the outside world looked more and more enticing.

He made his way over to his food dish and ate the brown crunchy bits as he ate he listened to the humans talk. The man sounded happy but there was always something hidden under his voice that Ouji didn't trust. Martha always sounded like whatever she had to say was so pressing that if she didn't say it now it would explode from her mouth. Samantha, his favorite, was always quiet, kicking her feet back and forth at the dinner table. She always did what she wanted and she was gentle and kind. She never yelled or stomped around and would always slip Ouji a few bites of her food when her parents weren't looking. When he finished eating, he made his way to the den. Smiling contently as he watched the humans stare at the talking box. He yawned and found a place to nap near the house plant, one of his favorite places, and stayed there well into the night.

It was pitch black in the house when the man returned. He reeked of a strong sour odor, permeating the air around him, as he lumbered around the den. He flipped on the lights in the kitchen and cast a wild look at Ouji, who was awoken from his sleep. Ouji darted for shelter under the spice cart. He knew better to approach the human when he smelled like that. The man stumbled around muttering things under his breath. He opened the cabinet door and took out a glass and slammed it loudly on the table, making Ouji jump. The man continued about the kitchen, with no regard for the noise he was making. Ouji thought if he left now, he could run to the safety of Samantha's room. So he poked his head out to see if it were clear. He was in luck; the human was drinking, and Ouji made a quick dash for the door. He ran but did not notice Martha walking in at the same time. Startled, Ouji headed for the trash can instead, as the humans began to argue. Thinking fast, he ran across the floor but accidentally tripped the man up in the process. Scott fell to the floor with a loud thud. He saw Ouji and scowled, reaching out to grab him. Ouji hissed and scratched him across the finger and made for the kitchen door and ran upstairs to the safety of Samantha's room.

One thing he would not miss was the humans downstairs. He thought to himself as he composed himself and hopped gently onto Samantha's bed. He kneaded and purred on her comforter. When she stirred he purred softly against her back, lulling her back to sleep. He was going to miss her, but he knew he had to leave or he may never get a chance like this again. He curled up beside her and drifted peacefully off to sleep. Perhaps, in his absence she could save another cat, for she had truly been a friend to Ouji.

Ouji didn't bother to make an appearance at breakfast the next morning. Instead he watched the humans hurry off from the safety of Samantha's bedroom. He liked looking out the window up here. He could see all the tops of all the homes in the neighborhood. They seemed to stretch for miles. He wondered how many other creatures were out there. Ouji had seen many types of birds, squirrels, and dogs of course, but the idea of meeting new and strange creatures excited him. He hopped down from the window and explored Samantha's room one last time. She had many animal toys. Ouji wondered how many he would meet in the city or the forest. Adrian said it would be dangerous, but in his heart he wasn't afraid. He was sure the mouse was just being overly cautious. Ouji headed down the stairs that led into the foyer and paused at the door. His tail swayed, making little circles in the air. Soon he would be in the outside world, soon he would get to see what lay beyond that wooden door.

On the day Adrian was supposed to return, Ouji could barely contain his excitement. He didn't care that his pacing was driving Scott mad. He ignored Samantha's coos, who eventually gave up and turned her attention to her toys. He even ignored his food. Ouji watched the window. He was nervous, but today was also a day the humans didn't leave the house early. He wished he could have picked a better day. He didn't want them to see Adrian, or worse, try to stop him. The sun passed the halfway mark and the humans were still in the home. Ouji was starting to worry that he would miss his chance but then he heard the familiar sound of keys being picked up. He rushed downstairs right as Martha and Samantha headed out the door. He stopped and twitched his ears, he could hear the light snores of Scott upstairs. Ouji wished he had left too, but ignored the man and focused on getting out. He turned down the hall upstairs when his ear caught the sound of someone scratching at the back door. He ran down the stairs as fast as his paws would carry him and turned and headed straight for the kitchen.

"Ouji!" Adrian poked his head over the edge of the table.

"Adrian!" Ouji hopped onto a chair and then onto the table. "I thought I'd missed you."

Adrian shook his head. "We were waiting for your humans to leave." He turned and behind him outside were two cats, one large orange and white tabby and another bigger brown short haired cat.

Ouji was surprised to see the outside cats so soon. He'd expected to meet them later. "How am I going to get outside?" Ouji asked.

"Oh don't you worry, you can leave that to me." Adrian scurried across the kitchen table and used the tablecloth to climb down to the floor.

Adrian headed for the back door. Ouji watched intently as the mouse worked. Adrian headed for the metal chain that controlled the blinds. He climbed up the cloth blinds, hopping onto the metal chain which caused the blinds to inch further and further across the door, repeating the motion, he used his body weight to move the blinds across the door. Once the blinds were at the end of the sliding doors Adrian climbed down and then climbed up the other end to reach the door lock and unlocked it. Ouji stared in amazement. Why hadn't he thought of this before?

"Would you give me a hand?" Adrian stared at the handle in exhaustion.

"Of course!" Ouji hopped down. "What would you like me to do?"

"Pull!" Adrian placed his tiny paws between the cracks of the door. Ouji followed and together with the help of the other cats, they opened the back doors just enough for the outside cats to come in.

"Nice place jack!" The brown tabby pushed his way through first, pushing Ouji and Adrian out of the way.

Ouji turned in shock and watched the boisterous new cat walk around the kitchen as if he lived there but before he could say anything he was pushed aside by the large orange and white tabby, "Coming through!" who headed straight for Ouji's food.

"Hey!" Ouji shouted.

The brown tabby stretched across kitchen the table, making himself comfortable fling his tail back and forth. "Calm down blacky, no need to get your whiskers in a knot."

Ouji looked at Adrian, who shook his head and sighed. "Who are you?" Ouji asked as he eyed the cat suspiciously.

"The name's Cheddar." The brown tabby spoke first. "And that fat cat over there is Puck."

"Hey, I ain't fat! I'm big boned!" Puck said as bits of cat chow flew from his mouth.

Ouji smiled and relaxed a little. He turned to Cheddar. "So you're outside cats?"

"Born and raised, house cat." Cheddar stood and jumped onto the counter tops, paying no mind to whatever he knocked over.

A plastic cup fell to the floor and Ouji jumped and turned around. "Hey! Not so loud." Ouji hissed eyeing the ceiling. "There's a human up there."

Adrian looked up. "Oh dear, then we must hurry then."

Adrian made his way to the door, but Cheddar pinned his long tail down with his paw. "Not so fast squeaky, you said that we get the final word in letting this house cat join our pack."

Cheddar turned and walked a full circle around Ouji, staring the house cat down like a hawk. They'd seen many house cats in their time who wanted to be free, spoiled little brats who were tired of their free meals and cozy little beds near the fire, searching for something more.

Cheddar wrinkled his nose. "Why does a little house cat like you want to go out into the big bad world?" Cheddar stepped into Ouji's comfort zone, baring his teeth in a wide grin.

Ouji stepped back but held his ground. "I'm tired of being trapped. I want to be free."

"Free!?" Cheddar bellowed. "You hear that, Puck? We got a house cat who wants to be free." Cheddar could not contain his laughter.

Puck walked over and joined his friend. "Listen kid, being free ain't all it's cracked up to be. There ain't no bowl of chow waiting for you in the morning. No bed made of cotton either."

"I-I know." Ouji ducked down as Puck and Cheddar circled him.

"Maybe you should stay here where you belong, house cat." Cheddar smirked.

"Now now!" Adrian intervened. "Ouji is aware of the dangers."

"O-u-ji? What kind of name is that for a cat?" Cheddar looked him up and down.

"It's my name and I like it!" Ouji snapped back.

Cheddar raised his brow. He had spunk, he'd give him that. "Alright, O-u-ji the house cat," he teased and took a seat next to the counter. "It's your death wish."

Puck stepped forward. "Now hold up, Cheddar." Puck turned to Ouji. "Is this really what you want, kid?"

Ouji nodded. "More than anything."

Puck looked into the black cat's eyes for several moments, and then burst into a wild smile. "You heard him Cheddar!" Puck laughed. "Welcome to the gang kid!" He purred.

"Really?" Ouji looked at Puck and Cheddar.

"Sure! We could always use the extra muscle." Puck looked at Cheddar. "Right Cheddar?"

The brown tabby huffed and rolled his eyes. "Eh."

"Right, Cheddar?" Puck gave him a look.

"Yeah, yeah!" Cheddar got up and crossed the room. "Just don't die." He hissed under his breath as he passed Ouji.

Ouji pulled his ears back as he watched Cheddar disappear behind the cloth blinds.

"Don't mind him!" Puck head-butted Ouji in the side. "You're one of us now."

"Excellent!" Adrian clasped his paws together. "Now we must hurry before the human wakes up."

The four of them left the house and hurried across the backyard. Ouji looked over his shoulder one last time at the back door. There was something about watching the house fade into the distance that was liberating and a little frightening too. No more meals twice a day, no more sleeping twelve hours a day, no more looking out of the window. He would finally be able to begin his life and make his own decisions.

The two cats spent their entire day showing the Ouji around. They told him which yards were okay to go in and which houses had mean aggressive dogs. They warned Ouji about humans and their cars and how it was never wise to take one on. All of this information was very overwhelming and Ouji wasn't sure how they kept up with it all as he walked with his new friends. Ouji did however enjoy walking through the soft grass and on the stony black road; it wasn't at all the texture he thought it would be, but he liked it.

"What about other cats?" Ouji asked.

"Oh they know not to come around!" the large brown tabby bellowed. "This is my turf."

Puck rolled his eyes and butt in. "Yeah, Cheddar thinks he's top cheese around here," the orange tabby joked.

"Think? Ha, I'm the king around here!" Cheddar walked in front of them with pride.

Puck laughed. "Right." He turned to Ouji. "Don't let his fat head intimidate you. He's a big softy on the inside." He winked.

"I heard that!" Cheddar growled.

Ouji spent his first night in an abandoned dog house in the yard of an elderly couple. Puck said the dog who lived here was long gone but the humans still put out food like clockwork every day. Ouji didn't question why the humans did such strange things and buried his face in the bowl. He chowed down next to his new friends. The food wasn't much different than the crunchy cat food he got back at home and didn't taste any better, but he was grateful. When everyone was fast asleep Ouji gazed into the night sky. It was colder than he'd imagined but the sky was crystal clear. He could see every star as they twinkled in the night sky. He fell asleep to the sound of the trees moving back and forth, next to his friends.

The following morning Ouji had to say goodbye to his friend Adrian. It came to a surprise to Ouji as he thought they would stay together forever, but Adrian too had other friends to see and promised to stop by every now and then. Ouji was going to miss his little friend, but he was glad they met. Now it was just Ouji and the other cats. Cheddar was hot headed and arrogant and Puck just seemed to go with the flow, mainly his own flow, whether it was digging through people's trash or meowing at the top of his lungs. Ouji was amused by their behavior, and followed along happily listening to the two carry on about their lives.

"So guys, where to next?" Ouji finally gathered up the courage to ask.

Cheddar turned and eyed him. "Aww house cat starting to get bored?" Cheddar teased.

"No, I ah?" Ouji looked away. He didn't want to seem like he was complaining; he just wanted more of a game plan.

"Wait!" Puck stopped and sniffed the air. Cheddar and Ouji looked at him. Puck jumped with joy and licked his lips. "It's breakfast time boys!"

The orange and white tabby took off down the sidewalk like something was chasing him. Cheddar followed him close behind. "You coming, house cat?" he shouted back. Ouji nodded and ran after them. Puck ran down the sidewalk for half a block, then cut through a yard. He jumped into a bush and into the next yard where there was a tall metal fence. He stopped and focused on the yard. For cats as large as they were, they were really fast Ouji thought as he tried to catch his breath. Ouji watched Puck check out the yard. To Ouji it was no different than the one they had slept in the night before. There were a few trees and toys spread about, even a little dog house, but pretty much the same.

Puck climbed the gray chain linked fence with ease. He walked the perimeter with caution, never once taking his eyes off the dog house. Cheddar followed suit, but stayed seated at the top maintaining perfect balance. Puck stopped and looked around. He squinted his eyes, focusing on something Ouji could not see. The orange tabby jumped from the fence into the yard. He stole looks between the dog house and the back door of the house. Without hesitation, he made his way to the backdoor. He was almost there when his paw stepped on a squeaky toy hidden in his path. He stopped as the fur on his back rose.

Behind him something stirred in the dog house. Ouji and Cheddar locked eyes on the small house under the tree. There was a low growl, then a bark. Ouji was scared; he was sure there was a dog in there. He couldn't move. Cheddar jumped from the fence into the yard. The dog barked and growled and slowly appeared from the dog house and Ouji couldn't believe his eyes. The dog was no bigger than Ouji himself. The tiny terrier ran straight for Puck, who dodged with ease. The dog was leashed, which confused Ouji, but only increased the grins on the street cat's face.

The terrier ran after Puck first but Cheddar lunged at him, scaring the dog out of his wits. Cheddar gave chase and soon had the dog running for his life. Puck rounded from the left side of the yard around the tree making the dog take a sharp right. The spotted animal ran around the tree only to be met with a surprise assault of claws and teeth. The dog yipped and ran around the tree like a frantic squirrel. Puck and Cheddar kept this up until the leash grew so short the dog couldn't run anymore. Ouji watched he wanted to close his eyes, afraid the two cats would eat the dog, but the two only pranced away in laughter, heading to the back door.

"Kid! You coming or what?" Cheddar teased.

Now could he see the cat's true objective. Next to the door was a large bowl of kibble. Ouji climbed the fence and joined them, stopping only to see if the dog was okay.

"Oh don't worry about him." Cheddar looked over his shoulder. "Dogs are stupid. Once they get tied around like that it takes them all day to figure out how to get free."

Ouji looked at the creature, who was scared and out of breath. He felt bad, but he supposed this was a cat eat cat world. He joined Puck and Cheddar and they gladly gobbled up all of the dog's food.

After breakfast the three cruised around the neighborhood. Cheddar walked out in front followed by Puck and Ouji. They walked until they reached a wooded area with bright metal objects sticking out from the ground. There were lots of tiny humans there, who ran and played. Puck and Cheddar avoided them, but Ouji was curious. He didn't see the amusement in jumping and playing on protrusions from the ground. He wondered if his humans came here or if this is what humans did all day, but when he looked up and realized he had fallen behind. Puck and Cheddar were nowhere to be found. Behind him he could hear the sound of children approaching. Ouji pulled his ears back, he was alone and completely unsure what to do. Just before the panic set in, he thought about what Puck would do. He thought about how easy it was for Puck and Cheddar to trick that dog. There must be a way to navigate this too. He just needed to think.

Ouji sniffed the ground. He picked up the scent of Puck's kibble covered paws. He looked behind him; two children were headed straight for him, but Ouji was quick and put distance between him and the kids. He looked back and the two children stood in the middle of the clearing confused, but eventually gave up and returned to their games. Ouji sniffed the ground again, but could no longer pick up the scent. He lifted his nose in the air and on the wind was the light scent of Cheddar. Ouji followed it and ran quickly for the bushes, running right into the big brown tabby.

"Watch it house cat!" Cheddar hissed.

"It's alright Cheddar, cool your fur." Puck relaxed under the shade of the bushes.

Cheddar huffed and decided he needed some air.

Puck grinned and stretched out on the soft earth. "Ahh, don't worry about him, he's always got his whiskers in a knot."

Ouji lay down beside him. He wasn't getting anywhere with Cheddar and he wondered if the outside cat would ever accept him.

Puck sensed his discomfort and broke the silence. "So, how you enjoying your first day as a free cat kiddo?" Puck flicked his orange and white tail back and forth.

"Good so far." Ouji said softly.

Puck smiled. "Good." He chuckled. Ouji watched Puck, he could tell that he was laid back because of his calm demeanor. He wondered how he came to be an outside cat. Puck caught Ouji staring at him. "What? Is there something on my face?" Puck licked and pawed at his snout.

"Oh no!" Ouji didn't mean to cause him to fret. "I was just wondering how you became an outside cat?"

"Became? Oh, I was born and raised out here, well not exactly here, but out here you know." Ouji nodded, going along with the flow. He didn't want to let on that he had no idea where specifically Puck was talking about. "Yeah, I was born out here and it's been tough, but I wouldn't trade this life for the world." Satisfied Ouji readied himself for a nap. Puck purred as he rubbed his head in the soft dirt. He closed his eyes and smiled contently to himself. "Hey, wouldn't you like to get away from this place? Get away from all these humans and houses and stuff? Live out in the wild? The real wild?"

"The wild? Aren't we in it?" Ouji didn't follow.

Puck laughed and rolled over to his belly. "I'll tell ya kid." The older cat looked over his shoulders to make sure no one was listening. "There's a place." He whispered so Ouji had to move in closer. "There's a place called *Ohajidi*; it means 'Paradise' in dog."

"*O-haji-di?*" Ouji never heard of that before.

The orange tabby nodded. "Yeah, they say it's the land of the kings. Somewhere far in the green forest, just past the city limits to the north. Founded by dogs, but home to all creatures, but tucked in there somewhere is another place." Puck grinned from ear to ear. "Another place called Lion's Rock, paradise to all cats!"

Ouji gazed intently while his big fluffy tail flicked back and forth. "Really?"

"I know a cat, he's getting others together to go up there. I heard there's no danger, enough food to last twenty lifetimes, and best of all there's no humans." Puck laughed. "What a place I tell ya."

"Wow! That sounds amazing." Ouji meowed.

"Shush shush yeah, sure does. I know this cat, Senior-"

"You ain't talking about old Senior again." Cheddar poked his head through the bushes. "And his crazy tales of Lion's Rock?"

"They're not tales! It's the truth." Puck turned and pouted.

"Hmp, it's all a bunch of hooey, all of it." Cheddar turned to Ouji. "You wanna get yourself killed, buy into that junk Senior jabs about and you'll get it for sure."

Puck wrinkled his nose. "Ahh, Cheddar you're no fun."

"That's because I want to live." Cheddar huffed and made himself comfortable in the soft dirt.

"Don't listen to Cheddar, Senior's the oldest cat in the city. If there's something beyond the city limits he'd know." Puck said confidently.

"Really?" Ouji looked at Puck. "What's it like living in the city?" He asked.

"What's it like?" A great big smiled formed on Puck's face. "It's like nothing you've ever seen and I've been to a lotta places." Cheddar grunted, but Puck ignored him. "I tell ya kid it's something else: roaring machines, buildings that touch the sky, fast cats, and good food. It's the best place there is."

Ouji stared with intrigue, he had heard very little about the city from Adrian and was eager to find out more. "So there are more cats in the city?"

"Are there? There are tons! And they all live in this big cat community, run by strongest cat in the city, Bucky-Myers."

"Wow." Ouji's eyes dilated.

"Yeah, I can see them now." Puck reminisced. "Ellie, Dipper, and this one gal..." Puck paused and smiled warmly. "Yeah, what a place."

Cheddar flicked his tail back and forth in annoyance, trying fruitlessly to fall asleep. "Sounds like a real cat paradise," he said sarcastically.

"Aww, don't be a sour puss Cheddar, I'm just answering the kid's question." Puck glanced back at Ouji. "Hey I'll tell ya this, the city has the best food your mouth has ever tasted, flavored meats in all shapes and sizes, crunchy snacks that would make your belly purr, and the best darn flavored water you've ever tasted." Puck drooled as the memories danced on his tongue.

"Mmm." Ouji purred. All this talk about food reminded him of the tasty morsels Samantha use to give him. If the city food was anything like that, he couldn't wait to visit there.

"Yup, paradise for sure." Puck rolled over to his side and rubbed his itchy back into the dirt. "Hey, did I ever tell you about that time me and my friends made off with the craziest chicken heist in the city?" Ouji shook his head. "Well settle in kid, because you're in for a treat."

"I guess I'm not getting a nap today." Cheddar grunted in irritation.

"Hey, I don't go interrupting you when you're off boasting in front of the ladies, so pipe down so I can tell the kid the story will ya."

Puck wrinkled his nose and gave Cheddar the eye. Cheddar grumbled, but did not say a word. Puck smirked and looked back at Ouji. "It was festival time, the greatest time in the city. Humans flock to the city like birds to ride roaring metal machines that soar in the sky, with bright vivid colors, and celebrate by preparing some of the best food the city has to offer. But this year me and my pals, we had this idea, this year, we were going to sneak out and nab us some of that tasty festival food."

"Why do you have to sneak out?" Ouji tilted his head.

"Because it was forbidden. Young cats weren't allowed to leave the safety of the community, because..."

"Because of what?" Ouji probed impatiently.

"Because of the catchers." Puck said dramatically. "The catchers were the biggest strongest humans in the city. They wore all white clothes, with big bone crushing shoes and ride around the city in black metal machines, scooping up any and every animal they see." Ouji gulped and flattened his ears. "And once the catchers get'cha you're never heard from again."

Ouji gulped. "Again?"

"That's right, but me and my friends we weren't afraid of no catchers back then, back then we were bolder than an alley dog." Puck boasted, puffing out his chest. "So me and my friends, we got together and snuck out, just a little before sunset, set on getting us some meat." Ouji nodded eager for more and Puck chuckled. "So we took off down the street into the main part of the city and boy was it packed. There were people everywhere, running and shouting, and stomping around. It was like dodging ice from the sky, but we made it to the back of the festival. Cause you see, in the back, that's where the festival folk kept their meat. They parked their carts and wagons round and left. Unguarded."

"Wo." Ouji's eyes expanded.

"Yeah, so me and my buddies we found ourselves at the gate of food heaven. Humans were standing around, but not at their carts. My buddy Dipper asked, how you gonna know which one got the best meat?" Puck smirked and raised his nose in the air. "Easy, follow me, I shouted, and I found us a hole we could all fit through. Once we were clear we put a step on it. I raced down the lane, sniffing every cart with my super sniffer. My friends could barely keep up! Then it hit me, I sniffed the air, just four carts down, I could smell the festival famous smoked chicken, a staple of festival goodies brought back by the older cats. We ran towards it, but just our luck it was locked up tight." Ouji frowned. "But we had a secret weapon, my friend Ellie was the best lock picker in the city. Using her brains we were able to get in and lift three huge pieces of chicken from the cart, but suddenly, just when we thought we were home free, a human appeared and with him was the meanest dog I'd ever seen. Our hearts popped out of our chest when they came shouting over and boy did we run, like death was chasing us."

Ouji tensed up. "Did you make it?"

"Heck yeah! I told ya kid, we were the fastest and the strongest cats around, ain't nobody gonna catch us."

"Wow." Ouji settled down.

Puck sighed happily. "Boy was old Fibbie mad." He laughed to himself.

Ouji watched his friend, but was curious about something else. "Why'd you leave?"

Puck's answer was honest. "Aww well, I've always wanted to see the world you know, mark new territories and such, but it sure would be nice to see my friends again." The tabby said before drifting off to sleep.

Ouji was captivated by Puck's story. He couldn't imagine a place like that. It sounded amazing. Ouji yawned as he settled in for his mid-day nap. He would love to visit the city one day, but for now he settled on traveling the worlds of his dreams.

Chapter Three

Dinner time in the suburbs was a lot different than dinner time in a home. Ouji thought he'd never miss his hard dry cat food or the wet canned mush but now he felt like he was on the verge of starving as he lagged behind Cheddar and Puck. They hadn't eaten since breakfast and it was now well into the night. Ouji wanted to ask where their next meal was coming from but the two other cats were too caught up in a heated argument about which queen would make a better mate. In what seemed like hours to Ouji, the boys found themselves in another park, very similar to the one they had spent the day in. It was dark by now and only the moon lit their path. Cheddar stopped and turned his head and hushed Puck and Ouji. He'd caught a whiff of something up ahead. Puck gave Cheddar a knowing nod and signaled for Ouji to hang back. Cheddar hopped through the bushes as quietly as he could, out of their view. Ouji wondered what was going on as he watched Puck who was crouched down low to the ground. Suddenly there was a noise, then a scream. Ouji lifted his head trying to get a better look through the bushes. Cheddar meowed, giving them the all clear. Puck turned and smiled at Ouji, encouraging him to follow.

"Nice job big guy," Puck smiled at his friend who sat proudly underneath the bird bath.

Ouji followed close behind Puck, keen to see what all the fuss was about. Ouji froze dead in his tracks when he heard a creature cry on the ground. He walked closer and to his dismay, before his two friends lied an injured bird. Ouji ran towards the tiny creature to see if it was okay.

"Hungry, aren't we, house cat?" Cheddar joked.

That's when the terrible reality hit him. They weren't interested in helping the little bird. They were going to eat it. Ouji looked down at the tiny creature, though the language was hard to understand, Ouji was not deaf to emotion. He could smell the creature's fear. He could see it in their eyes. Ouji stepped back.

"What's the matter house cat? This not good enough for ya?" Cheddar glared.

"Ah come on, Cheddar. It's his first live one." Puck tried to lighten the mood, but the large brown cat only grinned wider.

Cheddar turned his attention to the bird. "Well here, let me help you." Cheddar bent down and hovered his jaws over the little bird's throat and chomped down on the bird's neck.

Ouji heard it snap and was so horrified he thought would faint. He wanted to run as he watched Cheddar laugh. Puck jabbed him, scolding Cheddar for messing with Ouji, but it was too late Ouji could not sit and watch another animal get eaten. He took off through the bushes running as far as he could. These cats, these wildcats he aspired to be were nothing but monsters. Why did creatures have to eat each other? Why couldn't they just eat what's on the ground before them? It never occurred to him that something needed to die in order for him to live. The truth was a terrible thing and for the first time in his life he wished he'd never left the comfort of his home.

The night was long, but morning finally came. Ouji barely noticed the bodies next to him. Sometime during the night Puck and Cheddar had caught up to him. Puck opened his eyes and gave Ouji a sympathetic look.

"Hey, I'm sorry about last night." Puck whispered. "It's just one of those things you gotta do, you know, to survive." He could see the hurt in Ouji's eyes, but then he saw a small smell flash across Ouji's face. "That ah boy, it get's easier." Ouji took his word for it, but it would take some time getting use to.

The boys started early that day, searching for food in the early hours after dawn. Ouji didn't say a word; he was tired and hungry. He didn't sleep a wink from the cold of the fall night, but he didn't want to complain. He asked for this and there was no going back now. He trailed behind the others as they marched off into an area that was wooded on the edge of the neighborhood. Suddenly Ouji found himself in a completely new world. There were trees everywhere and no houses in sight. Ouji gazed around as he followed behind. Was this the forest Adrian was talking about? It surely seemed like it. The cats stopped at a stream.

"Hold tight kid." Puck hopped onto a fallen log. "I'll get us some grub." The orange tabby disappeared into the brush.

Ouji nodded, turning his attention to the strange world he found himself in. The trees were tall and stretched high into the sky. The wind blew, blowing orange, red, and brown colored leaves to the ground. Ouji watched intently as the leaves floated all around him in beautiful dance before settling on the ground.

"Are we in the forest?" Ouji asked Cheddar.

Cheddar turned and started to chuckle. "Forest?" The large cat laughed himself onto the ground. "You gotta be kidding me kid." Ouji was surprised. He didn't understand what was so funny. "This ain't no forest kid. It's just a green patch," Cheddar said as he shook the dirt and leaves from his fur.

"A green patch?" Ouji tilted his head.

"Yeah, you know. Humans use them, so they can run in, or play in or whatever they try to do. They're all over the place and beyond this is more neighborhoods." Cheddar pointed his nose behind him. "And through there are the black roads that lead to the city." He turned and pointed his head in front of him. "You can take this green patch cross the road to another green patch that'll take you straight there, but a scaredy cat like you would never make it in the big city." Cheddar teased.

Ouji looked in the direction Cheddar pointed to. He ignored the brown cat's words. Maybe this life wasn't what he expected, but he wanted to see all he could. All his life he'd dreamed of being outside. Maybe the city was dangerous or maybe Cheddar was just trying to scare him, but regardless, Ouji wanted to see for himself. He hadn't forgotten what Puck said about Lion's Rock. He liked the idea of not having to hunt and kill and live in a place where everyone was free. He didn't care what Cheddar said, he'd like to talk to this Senior and find out how to get to the real forest.

Puck returned shortly, meowing that he'd found something delicious the humans left out. Puck's voice held a warning as he lead Ouji to a clearing.

"Listen kid, you have to be careful around humans who give out free food. I knew this cat, they called him Chuck. He was a pretty smart cat, but his only weakness was that he loved food."

Cheddar laughed. "Sounds like someone I know."

"Give it a break, will ya?" Puck hushed his friend. Ouji chuckled. "He was brave too, he'd sometimes fight dogs three times his size just for a single bite of kibble." Ouji was amazed as Cheddar rolled his eyes. "Then one day Chuck was cruising around, when he stopped at a popular spot under an oak tree where humans left food. When Chuck showed up the food was in a small long metal box. Any cat with a brain could tell that something was up with this food, but hungry old Chuck went in anyways. As soon as he stepped inside the cage snapped." Puck spun around, bearing his claws. "And like that he was trapped."

"Oh no!" Ouji gasped. "How'd he get out?"

"Let me finish." Puck waved his paw and Ouji hushed and nodded for him to continue. "Many cats tried to paw him out but the door was jammed tight and around dusk the humans arrived and took him away." Puck shook his head. "That's why you have to be careful. Humans ride around in big white metal machines and pick up cats all the time. Take them heavens knows where. Not one cat that has been lifted from these streets has ever returned. That's why lots of cats have a system. Spots that are known for pick-ups are marked with an "X" and sprayed on, by the alpha. It's his responsibility to mark these spots to keep others safe."

"Wow." Ouji had a new respect for Cheddar as he looked over at the brown cat.

Puck stretched and pointed his nose towards the trees. "The spot we're heading to now is a well-known cat spot. The humans are nice and they leave good food too."

Ouji was surprised, scared, and a little excited. He wondered where the cats were going, but he was more excited about the possibility of meeting more cats. Puck, Cheddar, and Ouji appeared from the green patch and followed a dirt path down a hill. At the bottom was an old worn fence where a few other cats were gathered. They crawled under the metal fence and joined the others who were lodging around bowls of dry cat food and water.

"Icizes, Honey, Dawn!" Cheddar ran and greeted his friends.

"Cheddar!" They all turned and purred as they greeted the brown cat with kisses and rubs.

Puck couldn't help but envy the alpha life as he walked past Cheddar and the beautiful ladies. "Hey Phil, Hey George." He greeted two males instead, as the pair nodded towards them. Ouji followed behind as he looked at all the new cats around him.

"Boys, meet Ouji, fresh out the house. This couch napper ain't so bad." Puck said.

"Hi," both Phil and George meowed.

"Ouji, this is Phil and George." Puck looked back and forth.

"Nice to meet you both." Ouji took a seat across from them. He looked at both of the cats. George looked the oldest with his medium smoky gray coat that was patchy in areas and had many scars on his face and forepaws. Phil had a more angular face. He was a black and brown striped tabby with long slender legs and a short bobbed tail.

"Don't be shy kid, help yourself." Puck nodded to the food.

Ouji nodded as he ran over to one of the food bowls.

"Who's the new cat?" Icizes looked up at Ouji as he went by.

"No one important. He's just some stray cat wanna be." Cheddar scoffed.

"House cat?" Honey purred as she flicked her long golden tail.

"We don't get many of those." Dawn turned her head and watched as Ouji ate.

"Especially cute ones!" Icizes stood.

"Cute?" Cheddar hissed.

Icizes laughed. "Don't be jealous, Cheddar." She flicked her tail in his face. She and her girlfriends were curious about the new cat and walked over to meet him. Cheddar rolled his eyes and reluctantly followed behind his ladies. They were soon joined by Puck, Phil, and George.

"So, house cat ever been with a lady?" Dawn flirted with her big beautiful blue eyes. She was a beautiful sandy tan and brown tabby.

"Um, I had a sister," Ouji said shyly.

Icizes walked behind him. "Hmm, is that all fluff or is there some muscle under there?" she sniffed around.

"Hey, um what?" Ouji didn't know what to say. He'd never met such beautiful felines before and it was causing his heart to race.

George cleared his throat. "Now ladies, settle down. Let's let young Ouji finish his meal. I'm sure he's hungry."

"Aww no fun." Honey stuck out her tongue at the older cat.

"He's probably fixed anyways." Icizes added.

"All the cute ones are." Dawn said as she and her friends rejoined Cheddar and walked away.

"Fixed?" Ouji said with a mouth full of cat chow. He looked to Puck who avoided eye contact. "Puck, what does 'fixed' mean?"

"Ah. Hmmm." Puck opened and closed his mouth, like he was struggling for the right words to say. "Ah. It means. Ah, it's like. Ah, Phil you want to take this one?"

Phil shook his head, not wanting to be the one who has to tell him.

"Ah, kid its like." Puck pawed his face.

George stood and sighed as he stretched his furry legs. It was evident that no one wanted to talk about it, but someone had to and they had to explain it right. "What Puck is trying to say, or means to say, is that you no longer have to means to reproduce."

Ouji tilted his head. "I-I don't understand?"

George blinked and flicked his long patchy tail back and forth. He had known this to happen in many house cats and he felt bad for them. "When you're picked up by humans, they take you away."

"George." Phil warned.

"It's okay Phil, the boy needs to know." George continued. "When you're picked up by humans, sometimes you're lucky enough to be dropped off again, but that too comes with a price. The humans take you away and take everything that makes you a tomcat and they return you with their mark." George pointed to Ouji's belly. "They leave a blue mark."

Ouji pulled back the hair on his stomach and just as George had told him, there was a mark on his stomach, faded and blue. Ouji frowned.

"It's okay son, you're still a cat." George relaxed into a laying down position.

Ouji had no idea he could have kittens in the first place. He wasn't even sure he knew where kittens came from. He still felt like himself, but he guessed that was just one more thing he didn't have in common with the other cats and that made him sad. Ouji finished his meal as he watched the others talk and catch up on things. He thought about *Ohajidi* and Lion's Rock. He wondered what it was like to live there, more and more did he want to ask Puck if they could go there.

"Hey you four behave!" Puck joked as he watched Cheddar and the ladies walk off into the distance.

"No promises!" Cheddar shouted back as the ladies giggled.

The other two cats were lounging in the rays of the warm morning sun. Puck joined Ouji, who was sitting not too far from them. "You okay kid?"

Ouji looked down at the empty bowl trying to decide if it was the right time to ask about Lions Rock. He pawed at the ground and avoided eye contact, but he had to say something. He swallowed hard and looked Puck in the eyes. "Hey, were you serious about going to see Senior about Lion's Rock?"

"Shh shh shhh, keep it down." Puck lowered his head as he looked over his shoulders at the other cats. "As serious as the sun follows the moon."

"Really!" Ouji's said overjoyed.

"Hush hush!" Puck looked around and moved closer to Ouji. "Cats around here don't like hearing about Lion's Rock. They're non-believers."

Ouji nodded.

"It's kind of a city cat thing." Puck sat. He thought fondly about hearing stories from his father about Lion's Rock, the cat's paradise. "If you're serious, I mean honest to paws serious, me and you can get out of here and head straight for the city. I know where old Senior is living and I can get a gang together and we can go."

Ouji nodded; he was overjoyed at the news. He was excited about leaving the neighborhood and going into the city. Puck smiled and said that he would talk it over with Cheddar and they would head out as soon as Puck said his goodbyes. That evening Ouji waited for Puck to return from making his daily rounds. He was surprised when he heard a noise coming from the bushes. He turned and was happy to see that Adrian had come to visit him.

"Adrian!" Ouji purred as he greeted his friend.

"Ouji!" Adrian hugged him. "Tell me, how have you been?"

"Very good and yourself?" Ouji smiled.

"I can't complain." Adrian swished his crooked whiskers back and forth as he smiled.

"Listen Adrian, me and Puck are heading into the city."

"Oh my." Adrian gasped as he felt like he had led his friend into even more danger. "You mustn't. The city is not like the neighborhoods, humans are a lot more scarier."

"It's okay, we won't be staying for very long, from there." Ouji bent down to make sure no one over-heard. "We're heading into the forest to *Ohajidi.*"

Adrian's face lit up. He was familiar with the term. "Oh my. Then you're heading to my old home then. It is beautiful."

Ouji smiled with his big brown eyes. "Then you should come with us."

"Oh I couldn't." Adrian shied away waving his paw.

"Come on, what do you say? I wouldn't be here if it wasn't for you. You could retire in your forest far away from the neighborhoods."

Adrian smiled. "I do like the sound of that."

"So?" Ouji meowed.

Adrian eyed him and smiled. "Alright, I'll join you."

Ouji laughed. "Yes! Thank you! It's going to be marvelous."

"What's going to be marvelous?" Puck returned with Cheddar.

"Adrian is going to join us!" Ouji danced.

"Really old boy!" Puck meowed. "That's wonderful news!"

Cheddar rolled his eyes. "Ah good riddance." He huffed.

"Oh Cheddar, you know I'll never forget about you." Puck pawed his friend playfully. "You know you can always come with us." Puck said honestly to his friend.

"Yeah right, I like living, remember?" Cheddar pretended not to care as he grunted.

"Alright." Puck stood and looked at Ouji and Adrian. "We better get moving. Senior ain't getting any younger." He gave one last look to Cheddar before passing through the bushes. Adrian followed behind. Ouji was the last to leave but before he left Cheddar stopped him.

"You take care kid." Cheddar exchanged a serious look with Ouji. It was the first time Cheddar had ever looked at Ouji as his equal.

Ouji nodded and ran after his two friends. Cheddar watched them leave, wishing them luck under his breath. He was going to miss his old friend. The big brown tabby turned and headed into the green patch under the setting sky.

Chapter Four

The journey to the city through the green patches was exhausting and long. The nights were cold, the food was scarce, and the patch seemed to stretch for miles. Ouji was grateful that Adrian traveled along with them because of his amazing sense of smell. Adrian could find the smallest morsel of food just by sniffing the air. Ouji was a little envious of his friend, he wanted to be able to hunt and gather like everyone else. With time Ouji eventually got use to the taste of raw meat, as many animals perished on the side of the great black road. These were the only animals Ouji would eat, as he refused to take another creature's life. Puck was amused at Ouji's unusual stance, but nothing went to waste out here. As he sat not far from the road, he wondered what other dangers lay in the city.

As the days moved on Ouji became more and more in tune with the world around him. His senses of sight and smell were sharper and his legs stronger from days of walking and climbing over and under foliage. He could climb trees now with ease and pounce on rocks with amazing balance. He was steadily learning how to hunt too and though he would never kill another animal, he was good at finding water and places to sleep. Puck and Adrian were impressed at how fast Ouji learned. They were sure Ouji was well on his way to becoming an expert outside cat.

During the day, Ouji enjoyed listening to stories Adrian told about the forest. The ever cautious mouse warned about fearsome bobcats and the sharp clawed owls of the night. He spoke of the soft blankets of pure white snow in the winter and the fresh rains of the spring and cool breezes of the humid summer. Adrian's favorite season was fall; he loved to watch the leaves change and marveled at how they covered the Earth leaving the trees bare and the ground covered with beautiful reds, oranges, and browns. It was truly a sight to see, much different than the seasons in the neighborhoods.

The boys traveled down a long winding path leading through an area of fallen trees. A week had passed and Puck promised they only had a few days left until they reached the city. Adrian hummed an old song in a language Ouji had never heard before, but sounded familiar. *"Tamoji Hijiji, Ouji Dah Tiji, Oxciji Hitoma, Ouji Dah Tiji."* The song sounded beautiful.

"Adrian," Ouji mewed. "What are you humming?"

"Oh, it's an old tune I learned from the wolves." Adrian smiled from the comfort of his soft furry spot on Ouji's back.

"From wolves?" Ouji had not heard much about wolves, but from his understanding they were like wild dogs. When Adrian spoke of them he said they were like the keepers of the forest.

"Ah yes, very ancient tongue." Then it occurred to him that Ouji was a house cat and probably had not heard of the story of dogs. Adrian sat up on his hind legs and moved closer to Ouji's ears. "Ouji would you like to hear a story?" Ouji nodded happily.

"A long time ago," Adrian spoke in a soft wise voice, "Before neighborhoods and before cities, even before humans, there was a time where the forest was ruled by wolves. They protected all the animals who lived there. These wolves were as old as the tallest trees and had bloodlines that stretched further then the longest rivers. Some even speculated that the wolves were there before the forest, that they themselves created the woodland paradise as refuge in the time before order."

"Wow." Ouji looked up.

"Oh yes." Adrian smiled. "When man first entered the forest, it was a wild place. Not for a two legged creature who had no protection from the elements or no natural defenses to protect themselves from harm. However the humans were very persistent and pushed further and further into the forest despite having every disadvantage. The wolves took notice of their bravery and followed man in the shadows of their journey. Each day man was faced with a new challenge and each day man would overcome it. When man met the fearsome bear, man cooed it away with honey. When man faced claw-baring mountain lions, man returned with spears and chased them off. Man built bridges to cross rivers, dug caves to survive the harsh winters, built shelters from the rain, and brought fire to the darkness." Adrian rose his paws above his head looking at his two very attentive cat friends.

"This activity did not go unnoticed by the wolves. They admired the human's spirit and bravery. So it was decided by the alpha that man should be given a gift, one of loyalty, strength, and fearlessness. So man was rewarded with dog. Dogs carried all of these traits and more, and made the perfect companion to man. This honor was given to man because they would be the ones to inherit the Earth. Even after the wolves were gone, there will still be man and beside them would be dogs to protect them." Adrian ended his story, leaving both Puck and Ouji amazed. "This is why dogs are the only creatures who can understand the humans. It is said that they listen in silence to man's commands and guide them through the path of life. But that's just what I've heard." The tiny mouse smiled and sat back on Ouji's back.

Ouji's eyes widened. "Wow." Ouji was completely captured by Adrian's story. He had not met many dogs in his life time, but now he was even more curious about the wild creatures of the forest.

"Oh!" Adrian jumped and flung his paw in the air. "That's why your name sounds so familiar! It means 'always be' in dog!" Adrian exclaimed.

"That's right!" Ouji would never forget the name is friend gave him back at the shelter. It was truly a gift, one that he would treasure forever.

"You know, it could be considered a high honor to have a name in Dog." Adrian smiled as he settled back onto the soft black fur of Ouji's back.

"Wow, that's some story." Puck looked over his shoulders. "Gotta love those old stories, reminds me of my kitten days. Only in the city can you get generations of history, just by lying in the alley." Puck smiled ear to ear. "Let's break here for the night."

Puck dug a cozy little spot in the earth behind some bushes for them to sleep, while Adrian and Ouji forged for food. Ouji let the words 'always be' roll around in his mind. He was glad Adrian had recognized the word. Confirming the meaning behind his name grounded him. It gave him something that he could visualize and own, a place to finally belong. Perhaps there was no definition of the word normal; whether you were a house cat or a wildcat, maybe life was what you made it. Whatever it was, he was happy he was living it. He missed his warm bed on the coldest nights, but enjoyed the long walks through the trees during the day. He thought often of all those who had been in his life, no matter how brief. He saw his sister in the streams and his brother in the bark. He wondered if his mother was an outside cat and wondered if she walked these same paths. He saw her soft golden orange fur in setting sun and it made him feel like he was on the right path. He thought of Samantha and the kindness she had shown him. Ouji purred and perched atop a rotted log and watched the last bit of sun leave the sky. Who knew what new adventures awaited him in the city and beyond, but he was grateful for the chance to experience it.

A short three days later, they arrived at the edge of the city. They stood at the foot of the great green patch staring at the foggy horizon ahead. Ouji had never seen such a sight. The buildings looked ten times bigger than the tiny dwellings he once called home. He was amazed and even more eager to explore. Puck led the group as they crossed a vacant lot towards an old concrete bridge. As they walked Ouji stared around, wondering where all the grass had gone. It seemed like the further they traveled the more the soft green patches of grass were replaced by cold black stone. It was like stepping into a different world. Ouji looked up at the sky again, at the tall buildings that seemed to stretch into the sky. He wondered if he were to stand on one, if he could see the world. He kept pace, following close behind Puck. From the bridge they crossed into an area surround by warehouses. It was chilly from the breeze running through the yard. There wasn't a human in sight but Ouji could hear them in the distance, their voices echoed through the yard. Ouji passed one building, catching only a glimpse inside. He saw a shadow strike an iron rod and sparks bounced off the windows. Ouji jumped and made sure to stay close to the group. After they left the ship yard they walked through a small dirt clearing into an area with run down houses and lots.

"Shouldn't be much further now," Puck promised.

Ouji nodded and looked around. Ouji hadn't seen many cats as he walked right behind Puck. He was eager to meet Puck's friends, but suddenly realized he knew very little about them. "Hey Puck?" Ouji walked right beside Puck now. "What are the city cats like?"

"Oh they're awesome." Puck smiled. "True pals, through and through." Ouji nodded. "Yeah, we got a special thing going on, you'll see. It's the perfect place and perhaps a good place for you to meet a lady friend." Puck grinned suggestively.

Ouji was confused. "A lady friend?"

"Yeah, you know, a girl, a sweet heart, a partner."

Ouji still looked at Puck with a perplexed look and his two friends around him couldn't help but laugh.

"A romantic partner Ouji." Adrian spoke into Ouji's ear. Ouji nodded like he understood and kept on smiling. He knew very little about romance, but he could tell by the look Puck's face that he was thinking about something.

"Is there someone you like in the city Puck?" Ouji asked curiously.

Puck was quiet at first, which was unusual of him, but he lightly smiled and looked at Ouji. "Yeah, sort of, I mean there was this one gal." Puck's smile softened and whiskers dropped as Ouji and Adrian both looked at each other. "But that's ancient history." The orange tabby laughed it off.

The group turned into a rundown neighborhood, there were more humans here, but they barely noticed their presence. They were different from the humans in the neighborhood. These humans wore torn and tattered clothes and smelled of outside and sweat. Ouji wondered if these were outside humans or if that were even possible. Puck stopped suddenly and sniffed the air. Ouji looked at Adrian, who had suddenly become very uneasy when they first entered the city. Puck's ears twitched left and right, then without warning he darted in the direction of an empty lot. Ouji and Adrian scrambled behind him running as fast as they could to keep up. Puck jumped over a pile of empty crates and tumbled to the ground with a crash. Ouji dodged the tumbling crates and rushed over to his friend.

"Puck!" Ouji climbed the crates and to his shock found Puck laying in the dirt head first in a can of left open tuna.

Ouji rolled his eyes and sighed. Why was he not surprised. Ouji took a step back but paused. His newly sharpened ears picked up another sound, light breathing. There was someone hiding in the shadows of the overturned crates. He bent down and readied himself to pounce at any moment. The mystery cat stepped one paw out. Ouji let out a low growl. Puck looked up.

"Puck?" The light gray cat stepped into the light. "That you?"

"Dipper?" Puck let the food slide from his mouth, then roared with laughter. "You nearly scared the fur outta me!" Puck greeted his friend.

Ouji breathed a sigh of relief, relaxing his tense body. He and Adrian carefully climbed down the pile of crates.

"Dipper old buddy, it's been ages." Puck ran over to his friend and brushed against him. "What's happening? What's up?"

"Not much." Dipper laughed nervously as he looked over his shoulder at Ouji and Adrian. "Who're the stiffs?"

Puck turned and introduced his friends. "Dipper, this is Ouji. He's a new to the streets ex-house cat. That little guy on his back is Adrian. How's it hanging though? Old Senior still kicking? How about Garth?"

Dipper relaxed a bit but was still a little tense around the new company. "Yeah, yeah the gang is fine." He broke eye contact and stared at the ground.

"Good to know pal." Puck went back to his food. "Say, why you all the way out here in the docks? You visiting old Senior?"

"Nah, Puck, ah, you see." Dipper ducked his head lower. "Things ain't quiet like you left'em."

"What'sah matter?" Puck leaned in. "Is it the city catcher?" Puck shuddered at the thought of the city animal control.

"No, much worse." Dipper was nearly shaking, his ears turned back. "Puck, I'm in trouble, real deep."

Puck tilted his head and listened as Dipper explained. Ouji and Adrian walked closer to hear. "About a year ago. Well let me start from the beginning." Dipper looked at Ouji and Adrian. "Back in the day, there was an old cat named Bucky-Myers."

"Was?" Puck didn't like the sound of this.

Dipper let his head hang to the side "Old Bucky-Myers ran these streets. He made sure that every street cat was taken care of. He found shelter in the run down part of the city and formed a safe house for all the strays in the city. He was the biggest and toughest cat in the city, a full twenty-three pounds of muscle and power." Dipper smiled in his memory. "He walked the streets with a fearsome look, but his heart was as pure as gold. He built the community from the ground up." Dipper sighed in pain.

"Just under a year however a new cat named Koga moved in. He was a dark smoky gray stray from the burbs far east of the city. Bucky-Myers found him starving and weak and took him in, but Koga was never satisfied. He always wanted more at every meal and didn't like to do anything for the community. He stole and beat up defenseless house cats and scared his fellow street cats away from food. So a decision was made that Koga had to leave. That he could no longer stay in the safety of the cat community."

"Wo," Puck mumbled in disbelief.

"And you know you gotta be some kind of bad to get kicked out of the community. So on the day Bucky-Myers asked Koga to leave, Koga challenged him to a winner take all fight to the death. Bucky-Myers, against his better judgment, accepted the challenge and all the cats gathered in the lot for the fight. The old rattling can was kicked and the fight began. Bucky-Myers was able to hold his own pretty well and from the start it didn't look like Koga stood a flying chance, but the suburban cat was smart and sneaky. When Bucky-Myers stepped right into the right position Koga launched at his throat, biting hard. The two landed in a pile of wood, which Koga had planned all along. In the pile were sharp nails attached to the wood. Bucky-Myers cried out and kicked Koga off with his back legs. The surprise kick startled the younger cat at first, but when Bucky-Myers stood he walked with a limp. Koga grinned and circled the older cat like a hungry dog. Old Bucky-Myers took a final leap hoping to take the younger cat off guard, but he was slow and Koga easily avoided him. Koga scratched, leaving a bloody scar right across Bucky-Myers's face. He jumped again and didn't stop until the deed was done." Dipper said as his eyes lowered to the ground.

Puck couldn't believe what he was hearing. His paws tensed as he let Dipper finish the rest of his story.

"The ring was silent. The only sound was Koga's beating heart. He shouted to them. "Here lies your fallen leader! Join me or die! The choice is yours!" The other cats stole glances; none were strong enough to take Koga so many submitted and joined him. Those who disagreed were either chased out or killed."

"That's awful." Ouji said.

"Yeah, and it's my head he wants next." Dipper wailed.

"What? Why?" Puck took a step forward.

"Everyday, when the sun hits its highest peak, we grunt workers have to deliver food for the pack. Every day, and I did." Dipper groaned. "But I was hungry and anyone caught eating before Koga and his goons is done for, no questions asked. Now he's out for my head. I haven't had a decent meal in weeks. I can't take on Koga like this. What am I supposed to do? It's hopeless."

"Hey," Puck consoled. "We'll figure something out."

"I don't see anyway around it, Puck" Dipper turned and collapsed in the dirt. "I'm as good as dead. Dead cat walk'in, right here." He groaned.

"Don't talk like that, I can pull some of my resources together, we can-" Puck looked his friend in the eyes and sighed. "Well we won't get anything done with you on an empty stomach. Here, eat up." Puck kicked the can over to him. "You'll need your strength."

The group stayed in the abandoned lot for the night. Puck said they would head to Senior's place in the morning where it was safer. At night it was too dangerous to leave with the risk of running into Koga and his gang. They would just have to hold tight till sunrise. That night Ouji found it hard to sleep. He tossed and turned but couldn't find a comfortable position to sleep in. The night air was chilly and the random noises in the darkness startled him. He could hear the heavy footsteps of humans walking around and the loud clanking sound of iron chains knocking into buildings. He wasn't sure how Puck and Dipper got used to it, but the quicker they could get to Senior's, the better.

Morning came bright and early. Puck insisted they move fast. They made their way through the abandoned lots following Dipper who led them down routes where they weren't likely to run into any other cats. If Puck's calculations were correct Senior's hideout would be just as unpopular as it was in the past; he wasn't the most well liked cat in the city. Other cats considered him to be a little crazy with his wild eyes and crazy stories. None believed his stories and cast him away. Though it was on his terms that he'd left, he cursed the ignorance of street cats and took to a life of solitude, surrounding himself with only those he trusted. They reached Senior's old hide out in no time. He lived on an abandoned lot deep within a pile of discarded wood and metal.

"We're here." Puck shushed them. "Hang tight." He went into the pile, through the tiny entrance.

Ouji and the others waited patiently outside, waiting and listening for a sound. There was a crash, a meow, then arguing. It sounded like Puck was fighting for his life. Ouji wanted to rush in but before he could make a move Puck stuck his head out.

"All right! All clear." The orange tabby smiled and led them in.

They all exchanged nervous looks and slowly made their way through the tiny crawl space. It was tight. There was barely enough room for a cat and mouse to walk side by side. Ouji crawled through the space. He passed between specks of light that dotted the crawl space like stars in the sky. Dipper arrived first followed by Adrian then Ouji.

Ouji was taken back by the largeness of the area. The walls were tied together by rope and wire and on the walls were hundreds of tiny paw prints that seemed to stretch for generations. In the middle was a small pit with a lit up object that cast the room in moving shadows of orange. Puck and Dipper took a seat at the foot of a large pile of old cloths and rags. Ouji hung back as he was curious but not brave enough to join his friends in the circle. He wondered what kind of cat could live in such a frightening place.

The lights flickered and a great big shadow appeared on the walls. A large dark smoky furred cat appeared with one cloudy eye and one gold-brown eye. Half of his whiskers were gone on his large round face and he had a tear in his left ear surely from one of his many fights from his youth. His mouth sported one large tooth poking from his bottom lip which showed even more when he snarled. He looked wild eyed around the room and hissed and spit.

"Puck dang it. I know you let some other cats in here." Senior hissed. "Where is he! Show him to me, where I can see him!" the older cat growled.

"No, just me Dipper and Ouji." Puck reminded the older cat. "Just like I said no tricks."

"Lies! All lies; spineless, gutless suburban cats." Senior hissed, as the dark gray fur rose on his back. The older cat looked around, focusing his good eye on Ouji and Adrian. When he seemed satisfied, he settled himself on the pile of cloths. "Well you came here, what do you want?" he asked, not looking at any of them.

To Ouji he looked nothing short of menacing, but he wanted to get a closer look. He took a seat closer to the pit.

"Come here boy!" Senior looked towards Ouji.

"Ah-" Ouji bit his tongue, he felt like he was being crushed under Senior's gaze. The fluffy black cat walked slowly round the pit of light. He looked back at Puck, who nodded and gave him a smile for encouragement. He sat a few inches in front of Senior. "Hi-Hi." Ouji whispered under his breath.

Senior took one look at him and huffed. "House cat." Senior hissed. "Aren't you a little far from your home, house pet?" His old whiskers shook back and forth, casting shadows on his face.

"Ah-" Ouji stuttered.

"Come on Senior, he's here with me." Puck intervened.

"I ain't talking to you boy!" Senior snapped, turning his head to the orange tabby.

Puck backed off. Ouji would be on his own for this one.

Senior hissed then turned his attention back to the house cat before him. "I'm talking to you house cat."

Senior stared at Ouji in utter disgust. To Senior Ouji was like an open book, another house cat sticking his nose into danger only to slump back when things got messy. Ouji could feel Senior's judgmental eyes digging into his back and that made him a little angry. He didn't deserve to sit here and be judged. He had gotten this far and worked very hard. He felt a spark inside of him flare up. He stared back at Senior.

"Yes sir!" Ouji stood tall for the first time in his life. "Senior sir, we have come here to ask you if you could take us to the forest," Ouji blurted.

Puck, Dipper, and Adrian all looked at each other in shock. They watched Ouji stand his ground as Senior's look became more and more menacing. Suddenly the warm cave was as cold as a winter night.

Then a low growl from Senior's chest broke the silence. "The forest ain't no place for a house cat."

"Then I'll make my own place!" Ouji retorted. He had no idea where this sudden quickness of tongue was coming from, but the flare up inside of him refused to be smothered.

Senior stared him down for what seemed like hours, then grinned. "Puck, where did you find this ballsy little one?" The older cat laughed.

"Ha ha, that's my boy. Ouji the house cat." Puck laughed nervously.

Senior laughed again before making himself more comfortable on the pile of the cloths. He older cat groomed himself before speaking again. "The forest, hm? I already told Puck I'm too old for that stuff."

Ouji looked at Puck.

"Awwww come on Senior, we could get a gang together." Puck begged.

"No." Senior ignored him.

Ouji looked at Adrian. "Well, could you tell us how to get there?" Ouji asked.

Senior looked down at the black cat and laughed. "Ha, you can't be as dumb as you look. Tell me house cat, why do you want to go to the forest of all places?"

Ouji was taken back, he never really thought about it before. He did want to get away from the humans, to be free, but wasn't he free now? Ouji furrowed his brow. He looked up at Senior with no answer and the older cat grinned.

Ouji stared at the dirt for a long moment. "I want to go to the forest to find the meaning of my existence. I want to meet the wolves and ask them about the world and why all of us live here." Ouji looked up at Senior.

Puck and Dipper gulped, waiting for Senior to lash out.

"You're a fool, no you're an idiot. You want to go into the great woods and get yourself killed taking to wolves. How foolish." Senior grunted. "But. Only a fool would believe there is such a meaning to this existence." Senior stood and stretched. "You find some others and I'll consider it." He stood tall and grinned, showing more of his protruding tooth.

Ouji's face lit up. "Thank you!"

The older cat turned and grunted as he moved towards another pile of cloths deeper in the cave. Ouji turned to Puck. They were bubbling with excitement. Senior told them they could stay for the night if they desired, only if they promised not to disturb him. For this everyone, especially Dipper, was grateful.

Ouji and Adrian napped while Puck thought of a plan to save Dipper. He couldn't live with himself if he up and left without helping his old friend. Puck begged Dipper to run to the suburbs where Puck had friends but Dipper was afraid to leave his only friends behind. The city was his home, the only place he knew. Puck paced the floor in the cave trying to come up with a plan.

"Arg!" Puck hissed in frustration. "I got nothing." He sighed.

"It's okay Puck, you did your best." Dipper tried to console his friend. "Besides, I got myself into this mess, I'll figure a way out." The gray cat put on his best smile.

"That's it!" Puck put his paw down. "We'll just have to go into the city after Koga ourselves. You stay here."

"No Puck! It's dangerous," Dipper warned.

"He's not after me, besides we're going to need a whole lot of support if we're going to take him."

"Take him? Puck, there's no winning. You either follow him or flee and with winter right around the corner no cat is going to follow you into the afterlife." Dipper said.

"What about Ellie and Garth and Missy?"

Dipper sighed and slumped to the ground. "I don't want to get them involved."

"They're your friends, our friends. We're not going to let you be Koga chow." Puck smiled.

"Thanks pal." Dipper head-butted Puck in the side. He knew he could always count on his friends to have his back when times were tough.

Ouji slept a lot better in Senior's den; he felt safer in the darkness of the cave and dreamed happily of the forest. Puck left and brought back meat. It was the best meal they'd ever had. Everyone was talking; though Senior didn't join them they could still feel his presence. In the morning Puck planned to head for the other side of the city to where more of their friends were. It didn't feel right to Puck, leaving and knowing that the state of the cat community was in such great danger. Ouji had no idea what awaited him further in the city but in his heart he was prepared to give it his best.

Morning came, as the sun's rays rolled over the city, chasing the cold away. Everyone ate and left when the rays of the sun peeked over the horizon. They moved quickly in the morning light, taking care not to be seen by Koga and his goons. The closer they got into the city Ouji noticed there were more and more humans. They rushed about like ants in the dirt on the streets and in their large metal machines that rumbled past, kicking trash and leaf litter into the air. Ouji struggled to keep up with the group through the secret passage ways and short cuts. It was like navigating a crowded labyrinth full of unfamiliar sights and smells. Adrian was having trouble keeping up as well. He never liked going through the city; it was far too dangerous, which was the main reason why he never returned to his home in the forest. Ouji turned and saw his friend lagging behind and offered him a ride on his back. They turned into an alley and walked through a narrow path of hanging clothes and noisy dripping boxes hanging from windows. Ouji looked up in amazement, wondering what the insides of the buildings looked like and if humans lived here too. He wondered if humans kept cats in the city or if there were only street cats here. Ouji slowed down when they approached an area with a lot of run down houses where trash littered in the yards. There were few little humans here, only relics of what they left behind. Ouji stayed close and followed Puck to an old wooden fence. The orange tabby pawed a plank and it swung open.

"Through here," Puck whispered as he looked around to make sure he wasn't followed.

They walked quickly but quietly across the yard towards a small tool shed. It was run down, but the closer Ouji got the more it seemed to come to life. He could hear the sounds of cats talking inside.

"Are we going to sit by and let Koga run us out of town?" A female voice hissed.

Ouji, Dipper, and Puck entered the shack and took a seat in the back of the room. It was small but cozy, with bits of trash and metal nailed to the walls like art. The conversation stopped and everyone turned around. At least seven pairs of eyes were on them. Ouji slumped behind Puck and Dipper. There was a gray cat standing in the middle of the room, glaring at them, before they approached.

"Puck?" The female cat tilted her head and looked at the orange tabby.

"In the flesh," Puck replied.

The female cat smiled and ran over to Puck, both greeting each other with purrs as they rubbed their heads together. Ouji watched as the other cats in the room walked up and greeted the group.

"When did you get back into town?" she asked, then looked over at Ouji. "And who is he?"

"Ellie, this is Ouji. He's a house cat from the suburbs."

"Suburbs? You friends with Koga?" She hissed.

"N-No." Ouji shrank away.

Ellie looked him over. There was a strange air about him. She eyed the mouse sitting happily on his back in disbelief. He was a strange cat she could tell.

"Alright." She turned, walking closer to Puck. "We need to talk." She looked at Dipper.

The three exited to the back of the room, leaving Ouji on his own. Puck took a look back, silently apologizing that he couldn't be more social, but Ouji understood. He made himself comfortable in the back, as to not bother anyone. Looking around, he saw a large mix of cats, both young and old. There were kittens running around and old timers grooming and relaxing on the floor. Adrian clung tightly to Ouji's fur.

"Don't worry, I'll protect you," Ouji promised.

The tiny gray mouse nodded, but did not leave his side.

There was a creak in the wood and Ouji turned to his right, then from his left another cat pounced on him. They rolled, leaving just enough time for Adrian to jump off and hide.

"Hey!" Ouji hissed. He stepped in front of Adrian claws bared.

The other cat turned her head and stared at Ouji like he was crazy. "Hey, what's with you? You're the one with a mouse on your back."

Adrian hugged Ouji's back leg. "I know!" Ouji retorted, determined to protect his friend.

The gray and black spotted tabby looked at Ouji and then broke out into a fit of laughter. "You're a strange cat."

"N-No I'm not." Ouji avoided eye contact as his heart fluttered.

"The name's Jax." She smiled and sat in front of him.

"N-Nice to me you, my name is Ouji and this is my friend Adrian."

"Friend? A mouse? Wow kid, you're worse than the humans." She laughed.

Ouji smiled shyly and looked away. He had no idea why being around her made him feel like he had knots in his stomach.

"Are you here to help us fight against Koga?" She tilted her head.

Ouji hadn't decided if he wanted to fight, but he didn't want Puck's friend to get injured. He nodded.

"Good. Then you'll need to meet the gang." She turned and headed for the group. "Follow me."

She walked around the room and introduced Ouji to everyone in the group. The oldest cat was Fibbie, the mother of the house; she cared for all the kittens who didn't have parents and watched over them when everyone was away on hunts. She too was a house cat, but was abandoned by her humans when she was young. It was rumored that she was as old as Senior and twice as wise. Ouji stared in amazement as she sat regally in the corner grooming her long off-white fur. Next to her was a gray and brown tabby named Garth. Before the days of Koga and his ruthless rule Garth was a builder. He could make anything with the right tools and took great pride in caring for the house. On the other side of the room was a calico named Missy with spots of orange, brown, and black. She was a mother of three, two boys named Serma and Tama, and a girl named Uma. She too was like a house mother and kept a watchful eye on the kittens in the community. The last two sitting in the corner were a pair of black with gold spotted tortoiseshell fur. They were twins by the name of Bre and Brett. They were among the youngest of the group, but they were both very smart and expert hunters.

"This is pretty much everyone, all the other cowards tucked in their tails and followed Koga." Jax huffed. She couldn't blame them; they were all hungry and scared, but it didn't mean she forgave them either. "Just the thought of him makes me sick. Koga made cats turn on each other, steal from one another, even kill. Those acts were unforgivable, and that's why Koga needs to be stopped." Jax hopped on one of the boxes and looked out the window. The sun was a quarter away from its highest point. They needed to go out and get some food. "Hey." She looked down at Ouji. "In the mood for a hunt?"

Ouji nodded, eager to be of help.

"You can leave your mouse friend here, he's just going to slow us down." Jax said before jumping out of the window.

"Not a chance. Adrian here is one of the best food trackers."

Jax brushed off his comment as she stretched on the ground outside. "Your funeral." She turned and dashed across the yard.

Adrian smiled and thanked Ouji for sticking up for him. Ouji nodded and followed Jax out onto the yard.

Jax looked over her shoulder and grinned at Ouji. "You think you can keep up?"

"Well, yeah-" But before Ouji could get out another word Jax was already at top speed. Ouji took off after her. "Hold on, Adrian!"

Jax was able to get around the city with ease. She ran down the cracked sidewalks and through the back alleys like they were an extension of her own body. Ouji struggled behind, falling through the tops of trash cans and landing in tiny puddles of water. He was embarrassed as Jax stood above him and laughed. Ouji brushed it off, determined to prove himself. They reached the inner part of the city which was bustling with people and vehicles everywhere. Jax hid in the darkness of the alley searching for the best place to nab a meal. She focused in on a small café she knew was a few blocks down.

"Come on! This way!" she shouted.

Jax jetted down the street through the crowd of people who barely seemed to notice her. There was a sky bridge connecting two buildings together. She hopped onto one of the metal support beams and walked across without fear. Ouji was a little hesitant but he didn't want to be left behind or look foolish in front of his new friend.

Jax looked back. "You aren't chicken are you?" She joked as she maintained perfect balance.

"No!" Ouji stuttered as he followed cautiously behind her.

He admired her bravery. There was nothing like this where he came from. He hadn't even seen this many people before in his life. They walked across the sky bridge above the passing cars and people walking below. It was kind of cool being able to look above everyone for a chance. It was empowering and Ouji liked the new perspective. Jax hopped down and turned to Ouji and meowed for him to hurry up. He nodded and hurried across. The two headed straight for the back through the alley next to the café. Jax and Ouji poked their heads through the fence. There were a group of humans talking while taking bags of food into the café. Jax honed onto a bag of food she was familiar with.

"You see that bag right there." Jax pointed to the small pile of bags in an open box. "That's meat. We gotta find a way to get past those humans and get it."

Ouji looked over her shouldered, standing a little closer to her. He leaned over her which caused his long black fur to touch hers. He could feel the warmth coming from her and it was causing his stomach to knot again.

He coughed to hide his uneasiness as he stepped back. "Um, h-how are we going to get pass of the humans?"

"Leave that to me." Adrian smiled and hopped from Ouji's back.

Jax and Ouji looked at each other and wondered how the little mouse could help. They watched the little gray mouse scurry across the pavement. Adrian ran right for the box next to a large human and waited for the man to turn around. When he did the human shouted and pulled his hand back. The other humans shouted and proceeded to chase Adrian around the yard.

"Come on!" Jax shouted.

It was their chance to go in and take what they wanted. Jax ran into a box in the pathway, causing a human to trip into another one. Ouji ran around trying to avoid stomping feet. He headed for the pile of bags of meat, while Adrian lured the humans through the crates of fresh produce. The humans tried to reach in and shoo him away, but the only thing they accomplished was making more of a mess as all the fruit fell and rolled away. Jax and Ouji each snatched up a bag of meat and ran for it. They had made their way to the edge of the fence when Ouji noticed that Adrian was not behind him. He stopped and dropped his bag of meat at the foot of the fence and headed back. Jax stood there in shock; she couldn't carry both bags by herself and couldn't believe Ouji was putting his life on the line for a mouse.

Ouji picked up the pace when he saw that the humans had him cornered. Adrian cowered, prepared to take one for the team, when Ouji jumped out in front of him. He hissed and puffed up his fur. The humans jumped back, letting Ouji scoop Adrian up with his mouth and toss him onto his back. The two took off behind the fence. Ouji had never been so afraid in his life, but there was no way he was going to leave his friend behind. Ouji caught up with Jax who was hiding behind a trash can. He expected her to be mad, but she just looked at him and laughed.

"You're one crazy cat." She smiled.

Ouji laughed nervously. "Ah."

"Hush, I like crazy." She purred and tossed a bag of meat right into his face.

The black cat scowled, but Jax only laughed.

"Hurry up, crazy cat." She grabbed her bag of meat and was already half way down the alley before Ouji caught up.

The three arrived back at the old tool shed just in time for a late dinner. Both bags of meat were split up and shared amongst everyone. Jax bragged about Adrian and Ouji's battle with the humans. She smiled, looking him in the eyes.

"He's awkward on his feet, but when you really need him, you can count on him." Jax boasted. "We could use a few more cats like this one, times like this."

Ouji felt his heart skip a beat as he shied away from all the attention. Everyone ate and spent the rest of the day in the shed.

Garth took to the top of the shed to watch out for Koga and his goons. They were safe here for the time being, but they were being chased further and further from the center of the city. Sometimes things were hard and they struggled to find enough food, but they made it work. As long as they had each other, they knew they would survive.

Ouji was awoken by the sound of Garth shouting and running around. Something was wrong, but Ouji couldn't tell what was going on. All the other cats gathered around, waiting for the news.

Ellie ran towards Garth. "What it is?"

"It's Dipper!" Garth said, out of breath.

The crowd looked around the room.

Puck stepped forward. "Dipper? Where is he? What happened to him?"

"Koga's cats got him," he panted. "I couldn't stop him."

"Oh no," Missy cried.

Garth looked down, with his tail tucked close to him and ears down. "It-it was Trick and Unibar. Dipper went out, saying that the whole colony wouldn't be safe as long as he was around. They took him. I tried to go after him but Ox, Pete, and Q were there too. It was too many, so I rushed back here." Garth said as his head hung low.

"It's okay." Ellie nodded. "But we can't abandon him now."

"But every street goon Koga's got is waiting up at the lair. There's no way we can rescue him. He's as good as dead." Garth turned away from his friends.

"And so what?" Ellie hissed. "Who's next then? Are we going to sit by and let Koga pick us off one by one or are we going to fight!" Ellie ran towards the door. "You cats can stay here if you want and wait for someone to save your hides, but I'm not going to sit around and wait to die! We have to look out for each other, because if we don't no one else will." Ellie turned.

"Ellie!" Puck stepped forward. "I'll go with you," he said.

Garth looked at Puck he was tired of running away. This needed to end now. "Ellie, count me in."

"Me too!" Jax stepped in.

"And I as well." Ouji stepped forward.

"Us too." Bre and Brett came forward.

"Count me in too Ellie!" Missy stood next to them.

"Oh goodie!" Fibbie stood. "I'll watch the kittens. Ellie, kick that fat cat's butt!"

Everyone gathered to leave and headed for the door.

"Ouji wait!" Adrian called out.

"Adrian." Ouji looked down at his little friend, he could see the worry in the mouse's eyes. "I'm going to be fine."

"Oh dear I don't like this at all."

"I know, but we can't leave knowing Puck's friends are in danger."

Adrian sighed. He knew all too well what dangers a courageous heart could bring. "Be careful."

Ouji nodded and hurried to catch up with the others. Ellie was surprised but happy that everyone decided to stick by her. They didn't waste any time and headed straight for Koga's lair.

Chapter Five

Koga purred as he enjoyed his second meal of the day, licking his great big jaws as he ate his meal. After his feast he strolled around his domain and grinned. Today was his lucky day; his boys finally caught that no good food thieving runaway who had the nerve to steal from him. He sharpened his long claws on the exposed wood in the house and bared his sharp white teeth in a toothy grin. He turned his attention to his lovely company who was sitting and grooming herself by the window. Who was a king without a queen? Koga licked his paws and cleaned his face.

"Tell me my sweet Angel, who is the strongest cat in all the city?" Koga smiled as he trotted over to the gorgeous house cat, a longhair named Angel with pure white fur and crystal clear blue eyes.

Angel rolled her eyes. "Do I look like a mirror to you?" she replied.

"Ooo, feisty." He grinned as he rubbed his thick gray fur against hers. "Perhaps we should take this conversation somewhere, more private?"

She wrinkled her nose and turned to groom herself instead. "I think one of your goons is here." She lifted her paw and pointed with one extended claw.

He looked up and growled as his boys stood before him. "Well?"

Unibar stepped forward. "Ahh, we brought the cat Mr. Koga sir."

Koga's scowl turned into a smile as he turned and purred against Angel's soft white fur. "Excuse me, my lady."

"Humph." The pampered kitty turned her nose away.

Koga's tail shook at the base. "Don't worry, I won't keep you waiting." He grinned as he walked away, following his men to the backyard.

All the cats in the community gathered in the backyard. Tensions were high and rumors of a fight got the crowd stirring. The crowd split as Ox and Pete brought Dipper to the middle of the yard. There was a lot of hissing and meowing, but all grew silent when Koga stood at the door of the back porch. He walked down the wooden stairs and a path was cleared for him as all the cats stepped aside, heads down and tails tucked close to their bodies. Koga walked by, proudly showing off his big muscular body and sharp teeth.

"Welcome back Dipper." Koga spoke clearly, showing off his long white fangs.

Dipper's ears flipped back with his body low to the ground. "Look, I-I just came here to talk, to apologize."

Koga roared with laughter. "More like beg for your, life you slimy worm!" Koga hissed.

Dipper cowered. "That too," he added under his breath.

"You know what happens to cats who steal from me?" Koga stopped in front of him and waved his thick gray tail back and forth.

Dipper stepped back and gulped.

"They don't live to tell the tale." Koga growled.

Koga's loyalists went wild. They were hungry for a fight. They meowed and hissed and Koga ate it up.

"Let this be a warning to any cat that even thinks about betraying me," Koga shouted into the crowd.

Dipper could feel the situation heading for the worst. He made for the edge of the yard but Koga's goons blocked him. Koga grinned. He played with Dipper for a while, chasing him, giving him little chances to run. The crowd went wild, cheering on Koga. Dipper ran in circles but the other cats had him boxed in tight. Koga turned and faced the smaller cat. He fed off the fear in Dipper's eyes.

"This is it, cat." Koga lunged at Dipper claws and teeth first, and in a second it was over.

Koga had him by the throat, blood dripping from his mouth. He dropped the body to the ground and shook off the excess blood and dirt.

"Any other brave hearts wanna try me?" he shouted, but the other cats stood in silence. None dared challenge Koga.

From the porch of the abandoned house Ellie and the rest of the gang arrived.

"Dipper?" Ellie searched the crowd for her friend. The other cats around her recognized her and bowed their heads in shame. Dipper was laying on the ground next to Koga. It was over; she was too late. "You monster!" she hissed. She could not stand by and watch more and more of her friends hunted down like rats. This was not the legacy of Bucky-Myers. A fire exploded in her chest as she roared and charged at him. If no one would stand up for what's right, she would gladly take the job.

The other cats watched in shock as the smaller gray cat hopped into the middle of the yard before Koga. The fur on her back stood tall as she hissed, baring her claws and fangs without fear. Koga laughed, the look in his eyes daring her to step forward. Ellie jumped but with one paw, Koga smacked her to the ground with ease. She hit the ground rolling but was quick to her feet. She spun and landed a scratch on his nose. Koga was caught off guard. He snarled as he licked the blood from his nose. The nerve, he thought to himself as he noticed the other cats around him chatting amongst themselves, Ellie glared back at him. She charged, lunging claws first but Koga knocked her to the ground again. She rolled in the dirt hard, drawing up dust and rocks. The tiny scratches from the rocks were nothing compared to her years of built up rage. Koga grinned as he pranced around the circle. She wasn't done yet. The other cats watched intensely, not sure what to do. No one had ever challenged Koga and lived to speak about it.

"Come on!" He kept knocking her back, his size working against her. "You don't think you can win this, do you?" He grinned.

"I'm not afraid of you, Koga!" Ellie hissed, head butting him in the stomach and sending him rolling into the dirt.

He winced with a growl. "Don't think I'm going to go easy on you because you're a girl!"

"Bring it!" Ellie roared as she charged. They both collided in a ball of claws and fur.

Everyone watched, too afraid to do anything, too afraid to come in between the fighting cats. Puck winced from the porch; he couldn't stand to see anymore of his friends get hurt today and the usually mellow cat jumped into the fight.

"Hey!" Puck ran and stood next to his friend.

Koga laughed. "What's this? A tag team duo?" He roared with laughter. "A pig and a princess. Don't make me laugh!"

"If you're going to fight her, you're going to have to fight me too!" Puck hissed.

"Fine with me!" Koga lowered his head and charged straight for Puck, eyes dilated and teeth bare. He slammed into the orange tabby, hurling him into the air.

Puck landed hard into the sandy dirt and struggled to get up. Ellie hissed and turned her attention to the crowd around her. They were all standing around doing nothing. It made her sick. Most of these cats were friends and comrades she had grown up with, all brave and honest cats, turned into spineless worms.

"Cowards! All of you!" Ellie yelled. "Are you going to stand by and let this monster rule you? How many of us have to die to fill his fat stomach?" She looked around.

"Shut your trap!" Koga growled.

"I will not!" she roared. "I am not afraid of you!" She attacked him with everything she had, knocking him to the ground. If this was her final stand, so be it; she would rather die than continue to watch this monster rule over their once proud community.

Koga was quick to his feet and turned and swatted at her back leg, digging his long sharp claws into it. She howled and fell as she wiggled away. She turned and stood, but she limped. Puck looked up, it was over and he knew it.

Koga grinned. "It's over child."

Ellie stared at him with her fiery gold eyes, unwilling to submit. Koga laughed at her, ready to end the fight. Ellie's friends watched on, too fearful to interfere. Jax, however, growled; she was no coward. She didn't want to see her friend perish like so many others before her. She flexed her claws and charged, jumping on Koga and biting him on the back of the neck. He roared and shook her to the ground. Koga was growing tired of all these insolent cats. It was time to end this. Jax hit the ground but still stood and hissed.

"Hey! Why don't you pick on someone your own size?" Ouji shouted, joining Jax and her friends. He didn't come here to watch a fight; he wanted to help even if it meant putting himself in harm's way.

The mood in the crowd changed as the cats watched three of their own stand up before Koga. Puck stood and shook off the pain, taking pressure off his injured leg. He wasn't done yet.

"Yeah! You big dumb pile of fur!" Puck growled.

Koga snarled and looked around, more and more cats were starting to talk and whisper. Before long Missy and Garth jumped in too, standing their ground and hissing, ready for a fight.

"Fine! Fine! I'll take you all on!" Koga ran and chased who he could through the yard.

Garth and Puck jumped him. Koga may have been out numbered, but he wasn't out of steam yet. He fought them all. Jax launched to scratch him but was quickly kicked to the ground. Ouji turned and head-butted Koga right in the face, nearly knocking him over.

"Come on!" Ellie shouted, chasing him. "We're not afraid of you, Koga!"

Koga stumbled backward as he noticed more and more cats standing with Ellie. Soon even the cats who'd been cheering him on joined in. It was too much to take on at one time. In desperation Koga turned heel and ran from the yard as everyone chased after him. They all ran hard and fast as Koga ran for his life. They didn't stop until they saw a white van pull up ahead.

"Catchers!" someone shouted and everyone scattered, except Ellie.

She chased Koga down the street with such ferocity that she barely noticed the animal control officers pointing and gathering their nets.

"Ellie!" Puck shouted.

He shouted to his friends and they chased after her as fast as they could.

"We're not going to make it!" Jax cried.

"Leave it to us!" The twins said in unison.

They closed the gap between Ellie and them and pounced on her just in time for Koga to run right into the animal catcher's nets. Ellie hissed, but turned heel when she saw the white uniforms. They all ran back to the abandoned house, making sure they weren't followed.

All the cats gathered in the yard and drew quiet as Ellie stepped onto the front porch. She gazed over all the cats in the yard, all of whom she had grown up with. She stared at them not with shame or disgust, but with pride and honor.

"Brothers and sisters, for far too long you've allowed that monster to control you. I can not say that I forgive you for all your betrayal and cowardliness, but I can not condemn you either. Join me, and help me make this cat community the great refuge it once was. Join me and redeem yourselves!" Ellie spoke above the crowd.

All the cats looked around, but none moved.

"I-I'll join you." A tiny gray tabby stepped forward.

Ellie nodded and looked around. Others looked at each other, unsure if they should follow, but there was no falter in her resolve. Her confidence and self-assurance shone through and that alone was enough to convince the others. All the cats stood before Ellie. There was a different sense of belonging standing under her gaze, unlike Koga. She looked at them as her equals, she looked at them as family.

She smiled as all eyes were on her, showing her their new found commitment. "Go. Go forth now and tell the others. Spread the word that this cat community is alive and strong once more!"

Word spread fast that Koga the tyrant was gone and soon cats who had been in hiding started to make their way back to the community. The old abandoned house, emptied by the greed and selfishness of one, was now full of dozens of happy and smiling faces. All marveled at the sight, a once impossible dream, now a living breathing example of what good can do for a community.

Later that week all the cats gathered with food they'd collected. Everything was divided amongst everyone. Even those who were too young or too old to hunt, because it was never about how strong you were or who was more valued, it was about looking out for your fellow cat. That was the dream old Bucky-Myers had when he created the community. Ellie smiled as she laid down on an old worn couch and relaxed.

"Wish you could be here little Dipper." Ellie teared up. "But we won't forget you." She stretched and yawned before falling asleep.

Puck and his friends sat in the back watching new cats from all over the city migrate in. Some were old friends others were cats he had never seen before. It was a lovely sight to see, peace at last, just like it used to be.

"Puck." Missy walked over, her beautiful calico fur shining in the moonlight.

"Missy." Puck stood, taking in her beautiful form. In the mix of all the Koga business he barely had time to really catch up with her. He rushed over to greet her, trying to remain as cool as possible. "How are the kittens?"

"They're fine." She looked over her shoulder. Her kittens were playing happily with the other kittens in the yard. It warmed her heart to see them happy once more. Puck sighed happily, getting lost in the way she looked at her kittens. He swore she hadn't aged a bit.

"That's good." He smiled as he led her away from Ouji and Adrian to talk somewhere more private.

"It is. Things have really changed over the years since you left."
She smiled softly. Her golden eyes glistened under the silver moon,
melting Puck into a pool of mush. He laid down beside her in a soft
patch of grass purring contently. He missed his friends so much. He
wondered how he ever managed to leave them in the first place. He
loved the city, but mostly the cats that lived in it. Puck gazed at Missy
as she watched the sky. "Finally things will get better now."

"Hmmm." Puck nodded. "Almost makes me wish I didn't have
to leave." He sighed again.

Missy's head titled in his direction. "You're leaving? So soon?"
She frowned.

Puck looked away. He hated to break the news to her, but he'd
already made up his mind. "Yes."

"For how long?" She said, saddened, as she stared into his eyes.

"Well." Puck chuckled in an attempt to lighten the mood.
"Forever, but hey, you'll be alright. You've got Jon and the kittens."

There was a dark shadow that appeared on Missy's face when
Puck mentioned the name Jon. She tried to keep it together as she

looked at Puck, but it was apparent that something had gone horribly wrong. "Jon's gone, Puck."

"What?" Puck's face sank. "What happened?" He almost hated to ask, but he had to know.

"The catchers." Missy lowered her head. His memory broke her heart, but it was a cruel reality for the cats who lived in the city.

"I'm so sorry." Puck lowered his ears. What awful timing, he really wish he could stay longer.

"Can't you stay a little longer?"

"I want to, I do," Puck placed his paw on top of Missy's. "But I have to go, if I don't I may never get this chance again. Me and Senior, we're heading to the forest, to Lion's Rock, just like I always talked about as a kit."

"You're a fool, Puck." She glared at him, wrinkling up her nose. It was a fairy tale, a story that the older cats told to their kittens. She couldn't believe he'd want to leave and go out in search of a place he didn't even know existed.

"Ahh, I know, but can you imagine? A place with nothing but wide open space. Somewhere safe to raise a family and plenty of food to go around, no more catchers or more roaring machines, a paradise."

"Oh you're even more crazier than I thought." She shook her head.

"Maybe, but I believe in it and we're going to find it too. Come with us." Puck said unexpectedly.

"What? I couldn't." Missy leaned away, as her mind tried to warp itself around what Puck was asking. "What about the kittens?" She tried to find an escape.

"They'll be fine!" Puck insisted. "Just imagine the miles and miles of wild grass they could run in and trees they could climb. Is it not worth it to try, after all if folks are still taking about it, it must be out there."

Missy turned away. She wouldn't admit it but she was terribly afraid of the dangers that lurked in the city. With so many catchers on the prowl she felt she would never sleep peacefully again. She didn't want to have to suffer through that kind of loss again, nor did she want that for her kittens. "Is it dangerous?" she asked.

"What isn't, but the pros outweigh the cons." Puck looked into her golden eyes. "Come with us Missy, and I promise to take care of you and the kittens."

Missy smiled nervously. Her children deserved a better life and if she was going to travel, she would feel a lot safer with Puck. He always stood up for what he believed in and he was someone she could trust. She gave it one last thought as she started to purr. "Okay." Puck's face lit up. She might not have had an idea of what she was getting herself into, but she was taking this leap for her children, the most precious things of all.

"We leave in three days, just a little after dawn. Meet me at Senior's lot." Puck rubbed her cheek. "You're going to love it Missy, I swear." Puck purred.

The cats socialized late into the night. They were happy to have a safe place to stay once more. Everyone retired in the shelter of the old abandoned house, all except Ouji who took to looking at the stars. They were harder to see with all the light pollution from the city but when they did shine it was like looking at diamonds in the sky. Ouji lay in the dirt flicking his tail back and forth when he heard another cat approach.

"You were very brave today," Jax said.

He turned and jumped to his feet once he realized who it was. "Not as brave as you," he replied shyly.

She smiled and sat next to him. "The sky is really beautiful tonight."

"Yeah." Ouji gazed into the sky. "It's different in the neighborhoods. You can see more stars."

Jax looked at him. "There are more stars?"

"Oh yes. There are thousands."

"Get out." She laughed. "It must be beautiful."

"It is." He laid back down.

Jax looked away. "So, are...are you going to stay in the city now that Koga's gone?" she asked hesitantly.

It pained him to think in just a few days he would be leaving the city forever. He didn't want to tell her, but he had to. "No."

Jax sighed and sunk her head between her paws. "Figures." She smiled and looked up.

Ouji frowned, he didn't want to leave Jax forever. Whenever he was around her he felt like he was floating on a cloud.

"I-I..." Ouji stuttered.

"Could I come with you?" Jax asked, her eyes lighting up. "After all, you're going to need someone to watch your back, twinkle toes." She laughed.

Ouji's heart started to pound. "It would be dangerous."

"I like danger." She inched closer.

"You could die."

"Life is funnier when the stakes are higher," she responded as their noses got closer together.

"I-"

"Shut up, crazy cat." She leaned in and head-butted him as she purred against the long black soft fur on his face.

Ouji melted. He wanted nothing more than to have Jax come with him. He closed his eyes and let all of his thoughts float away and enjoyed the moment. He was sure Puck and the others wouldn't mind if Jax tagged along.

Morning came on the day Ouji and his friends were scheduled to leave. Others had joined them. Puck had convinced Missy and her kittens to come in addition to Jax. The last to join were Senior's grandchildren Bre and Brett. Although Senior wasn't happy about the idea of having this many cats tag along, what other choice did he have, it was an all or nothing deal. The path to the forest wouldn't be easy; it would take many weeks to get there and the journey would be long and hard. Senior gathered all the cats to dish out instructions and rules for their trip.

"Listen up!" Senior scowled. "I don't know what've been told or what you heard, but the road to paradise is not paved on streets of catnip. Some of you may not make it, some of you may even die, but your fates lie in your paws. Any who fall behind or are too weak to carry on will be left!" He eyed the room. "It is imperative that we make it to our destination before the winter freeze or we will all die." That struck a nerve. "But, if we stick to my plan, we will make it there safely, but only if we stick to the plan!" Senior growled. "Now eat quickly!" Senior shouted. "We leave when the shadows touch the den's entrance."

Senior outlined the path, giving them a step by step breakdown. They would have to move quickly and catch the train that smelled of pine and stop off at the place they are loaded up just out of town, where they would take the golden path to the forest. From there they would travel deep into the forest to where the river breaks and only then they would find Lion's Rock. After Senior's speech breakfast was gathered in haste. Ouji wished they had picked a better day, because it was cold and rainy outside. He hoped because of the weather Senior would reschedule, but when it came time, Senior and the others were already at the cave exit. Senior didn't bother to look back as he walked away from his lot. He'd waited all his life to make this journey and had no reason to look back on a life wasted within the confines of the dirty city. The group marched on in the cold rain. Missy's kittens clung to her and Puck for warmth, while Adrian rode on Ouji's back. Despite the rain the humans in the city still ran around in a hurry. Ouji wished he had one of their rain protectors as he shivered and held up the caboose of the group.

The day dragged on and the rain let up. They stopped briefly at a restaurant dumpster for lunch. They ate what they could and huddled together for warmth. Ouji had never been so cold in his life. He tried to hide his discomfort from the seasoned outside cats who didn't seem bothered at all. Protection from the elements was one thing he missed from being a house cat; nothing could top the warmth of sleeping in a nice soft bed at night, especially next to Samantha. The trip to the train yard was very exciting for Ouji though. He was able to see most of the city and all the diverse types of humans and animals that lived there. It was all very fascinating to him. On their first night they slept in an alley that had warm smoke coming from the sewers. It smelled terrible but it was cozy and there was plenty of thrown out food from the businesses around them to eat. It was late in the morning, but they made their way to the edge of the city to a humongous bridge. It was much larger than the sky bridge Ouji crossed with Jax some days before. Many cars and people passed over it and below it was a large slow moving river.

"This way!" Senior shouted as he hopped onto one of the steel support beams.

Ouji looked down from the support beam; it was a long way down to the water and Ouji wasn't even sure if he could swim. He looked up and Missy and Puck were already loading the kittens onto the beam.

"You're not scared, are you, crazy cat?" Jax teased as she hopped onto the beam.

Ouji shook his head. He had never been this high up before.

"It's alright," Adrian whispered into Ouji's ear. "Just take it one step at a time."

Ouji gulped and nodded. He hopped onto the steel beam and immediately felt the strong autumn wind blowing through his fur. He shivered as his heart began to race. He looked up, seeing that the others were already far ahead. Ouji gulped one last time before cautiously crawling along the bridge. The wind ran through his fur as the bridge creaked from the passing cars above. He had to be extra careful since the beam was still wet from the rain.

"Come on Ouji, hurry up," Jax encouraged.

"Yeah! You got this! Just don't look down!" Puck shouted.

Ouji inched slowly across, eyes focused on everything except the ground. The bridge rumbled and drops of water fell around him, he looked down and froze. He couldn't bring himself to move, his eyes glued on the rushing waters below. He looked up, toward his other friends already at the end and inched back.

"It's okay Ouji," Adrian encouraged. "Take your time."

Ouji tried to lift a paw but couldn't. He wanted to turn and go back but back was even further away. The others had finally jumped off the beam and continued on. He knew they were going to leave him if he lagged behind, but he couldn't find the courage to continue. However he didn't want this to be the end of his journey so soon, either. Suddenly, from below, a screeching howl erupted from a boat passing beneath him. Ouji bolted down the beam, all fear forgotten, until he reached the end, nearly colliding with Jax.

"Hmf. There you are, tiger." She smiled at him.

He tried to compose himself and smile, but instead he got a laugh from Jax.

"You are so weird."

The two of them caught up with the rest of the group who continued on. The train yard was located just outside of the city limits and getting there was no problem. It didn't take them long, walking over stretches of cracked sidewalks and green patches. When they finally arrived Ouji was so amazed by all the rows of steel and wood lined up side by side that seemed to go on forever. There were so many trains, some with hundreds of cars made of wood, others made with metal with black tinted windows. They roared and rumbled on hard metal wheels that sparked and screeched. How were they going to find the one that smelled of pine? Everyone looked to Senior who stood at the edge of the tracks, watching and waiting.

"How are we going to find the right train?" Puck asked.

"Silence!" Senior commanded. "We will rest here for the night and I will stand guard for the right train. Be ready to move on my word."

The group moved to a grassy area next to an old rusted warehouse. There wasn't much to eat, but Bre and Brett managed to hunt down a decent sized rabbit. Ouji reluctantly ate the rabbit meat, but was grateful for the fresh water that dripped from the leaky pipes. The group settled down in the long grass and rested. The urge to nap was strong, but they needed to be ready at a moment's notice, so they chatted to keep each other company instead.

"Mama, when are we going to go?" Serma complained.

"Soon, my love." Missy groomed her son, who squirmed and tried to get away.

"Mom!" Serma scampered away.

Out of Missy's three kitten's Serma, a black cat with white paws, was the bravest. He was the most outgoing of the group and the one most likely to get into trouble. He was a pawful. Uma, Missy's only daughter, was the little princess of the group. She was brave but prim; she enjoyed grooming herself and showing off her beautiful short white fur, with her long orange and white striped tail. She was the total opposite of the more adventurous and messy Serma. Tama, her third kitten, was the shyest. He was a calico just like his mother but pastel, with soft short light gray, orange, and white fur. He was Missy's little ball of fluff who stuck to her side like glue. She loved her kittens and groomed them as Puck entertained the little rugrats until it was time to go.

Ouji sat next to Jax and watched Bre and Brett nap quietly some feet away from them. The twins didn't talk much and didn't look much older than Jax but they both were seasoned hunters, a skill no doubt achieved from years and years of training.

"Hey," Ouji looked up. "Why are they sitting there all by themselves?"

Jax opened her eyes. "Oh, you mean Bre and Brett?"

"Yeah." Ouji watched from his spot next to Jax.

Jax yawned. "Oh, they've always been like that. They're kind of loners." She closed her eyes again, trying to get more comfortable.

"Loners?" Ouji brought his tail closer to his body.

"Yeah, you know, they like to be alone, keep to themselves."

"But why?" Ouji looked over but Jax was fast asleep.

He decided to keep quiet and continued to watch. He couldn't imagine living a life alone. They weren't truly alone, they had each other, but from Ouji's experience life was better the more friends you filled it with. Part of him could relate to the special bond siblings shared, though. He remembered the cold nights in the shelter. He remembered the comfort he got from laying next to his brother and sister. There was an indescribable feeling of safety and warmth, and there was nothing else like it. Ouji made himself comfortable next to Jax. He wasn't sure how long he would get to rest, so he took advantage of the free time to take a nap.

Morning came with the sound of blaring train horns and screeching metal on steel tracks. Ouji yawned and blinked in the fresh morning air. Looking around, he could see everyone except Senior. He stood and found the old cat staring intensely down the railroad line.

"Get up! Get up! Trains a'coming!" Senior shouted with excitement.

Bre and Brett were on their feet at once. Jax and Puck helped Missy with the kittens. The train slowed as it entered the train yard.

"All aboard! We're going to have to run to catch this one!" Senior called as he sprinted down the line.

"Run?" Missy looked at her young kittens.

"It's okay Missy! Jax!" Puck bent down and scruffed one of the kittens.

"On it!" Jax scruffed another one and Missy got the last one.

They moved quickly behind Senior, Bre, and Brett, who were heading for an open cart towards the back of the train.

"There!" Senior shouted. He sped up and jumped onto the cart digging his claws deep into the wooden floors of the moving train to pull himself up. "Come on!" he shouted.

Bre and Brett jumped onto the moving cart with ease, while the others caught up. Ouji picked up the pace.

"Hold on Adrian!" Ouji said just before he jumped onto the cart, tumbling onto it clumsily. "We made it! Sorry about that, are you okay?" He looked back at his friend.

"Just fine Ouji, thank you." Adrian picked himself off the ground and brushed the dirt and grass away.

Ouji hurried to the door to watch his friends run along. They were racing down the tracks next to the train but lagging behind because of the extra weight of the kittens. Missy was the closest and lifted her head so that the kitten was closer to the train. She held her breath and jumped onto the platform. Ouji and the twins helped her up.

"Thank you." Missy said out of breath.

"Jax! You're next!" Ouji shouted.

Jax nodded and picked up the pace. "Hold on little kitten." She mumbled before she jumped onto the train.

She landed perfectly. Ouji smiled with relief, all that was left was Puck, who was carrying the last kitten. Unfortunately the train was picking up pace and Puck was struggling to keep up.

"Come on, Puck!" Ouji shouted.

Puck grunted and picked up the pace. His large frame struggled to keep pace with the speeding train and they were almost clear of the train yard, he needed to think fast or he would miss their ride. He picked up the pace and sprinting towards the open cart, he jumped almost three feet into the air and tossed the kitten on board. The tiny guy landed perfectly in his mother's paws, but Puck fell hard onto the ground and tumbled into the dirt.

"Puck!" Ouji gasped, about to jump off the train after his friend.

"Leave him!" Senior stopped him.

Ouji panicked and tried to push pass Senior, but the old cat refused to move. Ouji hissed, not willing to leave his friend behind.

"If you jump, all your efforts will have been in vain and you'll both be stranded." Senior stared him down.

Ouji hissed as he glared at Senior, eyes locked with the older cat.

"Hey! What's-with-all-the-commotion?" Puck jumped up and down, keeping pace with the train.

"Puck!" Ouji cried.

"Hey-kiddo!" Puck smiled. "Little-help-here-please?"

"Oh!" Ouji, Jax, and Missy rushed to his aid. Puck jumped onto the platform, but was too weak to claim aboard. His friends were right there to help him and pulled him aboard.

"Puck!" Ouji purred and rubbed against his friend.

"Don't ever scare me like that again!" Missy looked him over for any wounds.

Puck smiled softly and brushed his head against Missy's face. "Aww, you know me, it's going to take a lot more than a little barrel roll to keep me down." He chuckled as the others purred.

Ouji turned and looked at Senior from afar. If it weren't for Puck none of them would be on this journey. Ouji was angry that Senior could toss a friend aside so quickly without a second thought. Jax walked up behind him and purred against his shoulder. He sighed and tried to push the events of the day from his mind. They still had a long way to go, but he didn't trust Senior as much as before.

Life on the train was hard. The nights were cold and there was barely any food around. They survived the days by searching for food when the train stopped at other train yards. They'd take turns hunting and gathering in groups of two, but even then they would go on for days without food. During the long hours of the day Ouji and the others spent time exploring the train, hopping from cart to cart; it was dangerous but it helped pass the time. When night fell everyone huddled up, even Bre and Brett joining them for warmth against the chill.

On the twelfth day Senior called the group in for an update discussing the next few legs of the journey. When the meeting adjourned Ouji went off on his own. He wanted to see more of the train. He loved sitting in the open watching the scenery go by. It was one of his favorite things to do, a habit he had picked up as a younger cat. Ouji enjoyed watching the terrain transform before his eyes. He saw wide plains of long grass planted in rows, places Adrian called farms, and pastures of large grass-eating animals called cows. It was amazing, a sight to see. He jumped on a few empty crates and headed to the next car. He was hungry but his sense of curiosity outweighed his growling stomach. He poked his head out of the moving train. The landscape had changed from tall buildings and houses to miles of farms and bare earth. In the distance he could see the peaks of mountains. They looked so small from here, but according to Adrian they were taller than the highest skyscrapers in the city. He looked down and watched the metal wheels spin and spark on the steel tracks. The noise was frightening and entrancing at the same time. He felt he could be up here all day.

"Going out?" Jax's voice scared Ouji out of his wits.

"Oh! Oh, yes. I'm sorry." Ouji stepped out across the metal support link that held the two cars together.

"You seem a little off, everything alright?" Jax eyed Ouji suspiciously.

"I-I'm fine," Ouji lied.

"Right." Jax laughed. "If you hold it in, your head might explode." She jumped out in front and walked to the next car.

She was right, but Ouji wasn't ready to tell and he didn't want to think about it either. The train was very long, about fifty cars, but Senior warned them not to venture too close to the front because that's where the humans were. Jax wasn't afraid. She'd been around humans all her life; she knew how to get around without being seen. Ouji followed behind her, being extra careful when crossing from one cart to another.

"Don't you think we should head back?" Ouji said when he realized they were heading to the front of the train.

"Why?" Jax looked back.

Ouji stopped. What good was it trying to convince Jax to listen to him? Really, he was just as curious about going to the front of the train as she was. Though they had been on the train for a little over a week, no one except Senior, Bre, and Brett had seen the front. Ouji wished he had Adrian here with him to scope out the place but the little gray mouse was fast sleep along with Puck, Missy, and the kittens. Jax made her way to the fourth cart; this was the closest they'd ever gone.

"Wait!" She froze and sniffed the air. "I smell food!" Jax shouted.

"What?" Ouji's eyes widened.

"Come on! This way!" She jumped onto the support link and climbed into the window.

What she found amazed her. This was where the humans who controlled the train lived. There was a little bed, with a sleeping human in it and a table, but best of all there was food. Jax and Ouji jumped onto the floor, being careful not to make a sound as they walked over to the crate of dried meats and fruit.

"Wow Ouji we really hit the jackpot." Jax meowed and turned and looked at Ouji who nodded.

"Come on, we have to grab some and take it back to the others." Jax flipped open the box with her nose.

"Right!" Ouji followed, but turned when he smelled a familiar scent.

"What are you doing up here?" Bre glared at them as she walked around the corner of the human's bed.

Jax turned. "We found food!"

Bre looked pass Jax at the food. "I see." She paused before she spoke again as if she was thinking about what to say next.

Jax smiled and looked back at the food. "I'm going to take some back for the others."

Bre stared at her as if she was annoyed, but did not say a word. Ouji was put off by her odd reaction, but his mood quickly changed when Bre agreed to help take the food back to the others. They carried enough back to fill all their empty stomachs, which put everyone in a cheerful mood. Everyone ate together, even Senior, but he was quiet throughout the meal. He sat there eating in silence, occasionally glaring around the room. Ouji thought it was odd, but didn't dwell on it for long. He was finally having a real meal; he would sleep well tonight.

Ouji awoke from his mid-day nap to find that Jax was gone. She had fallen asleep next to him and Adrian, but as Ouji scanned the car she was nowhere to be found. Ouji nudged Adrian awake to let him know he would be leaving, to which Adrian replied with a sleepy smile. Ouji looked around one last time before standing up and giving his legs a good stretch, shaking the rest of the sleep away. Upon closer inspection he realized that the twins were gone too, but everyone else was sleeping peacefully. Feeling satisfied with the safety of his friends, he returned to his mission of searching for Jax. Not sure which direction she went Ouji decided to follow his gut and headed towards the back of the train and to his surprise he was correct. He found her gazing out of an open door, at the slowly moving pastures going by. He smiled to himself, content on just watching her, before lifting his paw to walk towards her.

"Don't even think about sneaking up on me. I can hear your noisy paws from a mile away." She turned and smirked at him. Ouji laughed a little and joined her in the opening on the car door. "Isn't it beautiful? I've never seen so much green in my entire life."

Ouji too was amazed at the dynamic change in the environment. "It's much more than the neighborhoods that's for sure."

"Oh? I wouldn't know, I've never been outside the city before."

Ouji was surprised by her answer, then it suddenly occurred to him that he knew very little about Jax. He felt a little embarrassed that he never asked or mustered up the courage too. "Hey Jax, how was it like living in the city?"

"Oh it was great." Jax responded as she continued to watch the scenery go by.

"Really? Did you have any brothers or sisters?"

"Nope, I was found." She said quiet cheerfully, which surprised Ouji a bit.

"Oh." Ouji frowned, it made him a little sad to find out that Jax grew up all alone.

"What?" She eyed him suspiciously.

"Well, you said you were found."

"Yeah? What's wrong with that?"

"Well, um, you didn't have a family." Ouji averted his eyes, he didn't want to make things awkward for Jax.

"I had a family." She laughed at the confused look on Ouji's face. "I was found by my dad Gato, well my community dad. He was like a father to me. He use to tease me all the time and call me his little sound box because of my meow."

"Your meow?" Ouji tilted his head.

Jax nodded. "Yes, that's how he found me. He said that I was the loudest kitten he had ever heard."

"Wow, he sounds like a really nice guy."

"He was." Jax grew quiet and gazed out at the pasting pastures. Ouji felt a little bad about bringing up such painful memories. He figured it didn't matter where you came from, life gave and took, and it was something you had to deal with. Ouji sat quietly next to Jax, trying to think of something to lighten the mood, then he perked up his ears.

"Hey, how'd you get your name?"

Jax turned to him. "My name?" Ouji nodded. "Oh, you mean is there something special about it?"

"Yeah?"

"Well sort, my dad named me after his best friend Jack and his buddies teased him for calling me that, so he changed it to Jax."

"That's really cool, Jack must have been an amazing cat."

Jax shrugged, then laughed. "Well, he's not has great as Gato, but he sure was loud." A great big smiled formed on Jax's face as she reminisced. Ouji laughed with her, as she carried on talking about stories from her childhood. It was so unlike Jax to open up like this and to sit here and listen to her. It made Ouji feel very special.

Morning broke as the sun made its way through the cracks of the car. Floating on the air was the scent of pine and freshly chopped wood. The group woke, feeling the train slow to a stop. Senior rose and walked to the door, looking out at the piles of chopped wood.

"We're here!" He turned and shouted.

Everyone scampered up to the door. The air was fresh and thick with the smell of oak and pine. The train slowed to a crawl before it stopped in a train yard full of wood chips. Senior hopped down first and the others followed. He ran up ahead to an old dirt road. He looked both ways before sniffing the air. When the others caught up they found him staring eagerly down the long path.

"The golden path!" Senior's eyes dilated with joy.

"Wow." Puck looked down the path.

"Let's not waste any time." Senior marched forward, his excitement putting an extra pep in his step. He was finally making the progress he needed.

"Wait, don't you think we should find something to eat first?" Ouji suggested.

"Yeah. I'm starving," Puck added.

"Mama, when are we going to eat?" Uma complained.

Senior twitched his whiskers back and forth, but he too was hungry. "Alright!" The older cat grunted. "We'll rest here, but only for a few hours. I want to get on the road as soon as possible."

"Thanks pal," Puck meowed.

The kittens cheered and the group broke up to hunt for breakfast. Ouji and Jax left to find water, Bre and Brett went in search of food, and Puck and Missy looked for a place to rest, leaving Senior with the kittens alone.

"When do you think we'll get there?" Serma asked impatiently.

Senior glared at the tiny black kitten, who seemed unfazed by his fearsome look. "When we get there."

"And when is that?" Serma bugged.

"When we arrive." Senior shut his eyes, fighting off a headache.

"And when is that?" Serma meowed in Senior's ear as he jumped and played on his back.

"Silence you pest!" Senior roared.

Serma jumped and ran over to his brother and sister.

"What a grouch." Uma turned up her nose.

Serma looked back and stuck out his tongue. "Yeah."

"I-I don't know guys, maybe we should have stayed with mom." Tama hid behind his brother.

"Oh you baby!" Uma teased as she pounced on her brother.

The sunset over the grassy fields of the train yard, everyone settled down for the night except for Senior. He stared up into the night sky, impatiently waiting for morning to come. He loathed wasting time. He was too old for this. The train they rode in on started up again carrying its load of freshly cut logs, blowing its horn and pumping thick white smoke into the air. He turned and looked at the sleeping group and wondered why he hadn't done this trip by himself years ago. Someone stirred, but Senior did not need to turn and look to know who it was.

"If I should need you, can I trust you and your brother?" Senior looked at his granddaughter.

"Yes, grandfather. Whatever you wish is our command." Bre said without falter.

The old cat grinned. "Good."

Morning came and the group was up bright and early. Senior was determined to get on the road as soon as possible which meant breakfast boiled down to a few sips of water. The golden path was actually a very long dirt road. The dirt was a sandy brown, littered with little rocks and patches of grass. It was a place without many buildings and even fewer humans. Ouji wondered how such untouched land could exist. The sun shone high in the sky and though it wasn't warm it was still nice with a light breeze that swept across the land. Ouji watched the tall grass sway as small four-legged reptiles scampered by. It was beautiful. The first thing he noticed about this place was the peaceful silence. He could actually hear the sound of his paws on the ground and the air was so fresh and smelled of freshly chopped wood and churned earth. It was much different than the quietness and greenery of the neighborhoods. He wondered if this was what the world was like before humans or if he had stepped off the train and into a different world entirely.

Senior kept the pace with Bre and Brett not far behind. Puck and Missy kept up the rear while the kittens jumped and played around them. Serma weaved through the long grass without fear up ahead of his siblings. Uma sniffed the grass with disinterest; she thought the long green blades were offensive and boring and settled for walking next to her brother. Little Tama stuck close to his mom where he felt safe. He wasn't having fun on this journey; everything was changing so fast. He wished he could just turn around and go home. Serma jumped and played and hunted whatever insects he could find. The little black kitten hid in the grass, tucking his head down to his white paws as he prepared to jump on a gray moth. He waited until the right moment then lunged into the air. The moth easily dodged the little kitten's attempt and Serma landed hard in the dirt and rolled. From the edge of the grass Uma laughed.

Serma looked up and huffed. "Like you can do better!"

"I don't chase bugs." Uma pranced away waving her tail in the air.

Serma hissed and charged after his sister. Uma saw him and ran ahead and the two ran all the way up to Jax and Ouji. Ouji smiled as he watched the two play, their playfulness reminding him of his brother and sister. Out of the corner of his eye, he noticed a twinkle in Jax's eyes as she watched the kits play as well. Ouji wondered if she wanted kittens of her own, but the more he thought about it, the more his stomach turned into knots. Some part of him wanted to see her and her kittens play and be loved. Of course, he'd found out he couldn't have kittens, but he never really knew where they came from either. Jax must have picked up on his distress because when he looked up she was staring right at him.

"What's on your mind?" she asked.

"Oh nothing." Ouji turned away.

She stopped. "Ouji."

He looked back at her. "It's nothing."

"Right." She glared and walked away.

Ouji didn't like to keep all his feelings bottled up inside of him. They were hard to explain and made him feel uncomfortable, but he didn't know how to convey how he felt because he had never felt this way before. He lowered his head and sighed.

"Lady troubles?" Adrian, who Ouji thought had been sleeping, whispered into his ear.

"I'm not sure." Ouji frowned, letting his tail drag low behind him.

"Lets see, does it have something to do with a certain green eyed tabby?" Adrian asked.

Of course Adrian would figure it out. Ouji was sure that Adrian knew everything. Trying to find the right words, Ouji looked up at his friend. "It's that obvious?" Ouji chuckled and sighed. "I see Jax looking at the kittens playing and I wonder if she wants kittens and I want to see her have kittens, but I don't know anything about kittens. I mean, how are they made, where do they come from? I just want to see her smile. It makes me happy when she does." Ouji blurted out as Jax teased and played with Serma and Uma up a head.

Adrian smiled and chuckled. "Oh Ouji my friend, what you are feeling is normal. It's your heart."

"My heart?" Ouji looked at his chest.

Adrian smiled. "No not physically, but emotionally. You're falling in love, Ouji."

"Love?"

"Yes." Adrian spoke kindly. "As for your other question." Adrian whispered into Ouji's ear.

Ouji listened intently. "Oh! Oh? Oh, I see?" Ouji frowned again.

Adrian patted his friend on the back. "Don't be sad, Ouji. If it is love, then she will not care." Ouji sighed. "But she'll never know if you keep shutting her out." Adrian said as he moved from Ouji's head to his back to make himself more comfortable on Ouji's soft black fur.

Adrian was right, he should be more open with Jax. She was very caring and he didn't want to chase her away. Ouji thanked Adrian for listening to him, he was grateful for a friend that he could talk to when things got tough. Ouji rushed forward and caught up with Jax.

"Room for one more?" Ouji smiled.

Jax turned and saw him, his smile put her worries at ease. "I don't know, we don't want to catch your crazy." Jax teased as the kittens played around her.

"It's okay, because it's only transferred by bite!" Ouji smiled a toothy grin.

Ouji stared her in the eyes and the knots in his stomach started to subside. Jax laughed and pawed him in the face.

"Alright crazy cat, lets see what you got." She took off with the kittens.

The day was long and grueling and everyone was exhausted when they finally arrived at a small town on the edge of the forest and decided to stay there for the night. The sun was setting, painting an orange glow on all the old buildings and shops around them. They walked on the side of the road, where they were safe from the trucks passing by hauling freshly cut wood. Around them were rows of rustic shops and taverns. It was nothing like the city, with its faded cracked roads and its tiny shops and buildings. It was a world of its own, tucked away next to the forest. They searched for shelter and food and were lucky to find both in the back of a small diner.

"This will do." Senior surveyed the thick brush. He turned to Bre and Brett and without speaking sent them off to search for food.

"Cozy." Puck joked as he made his way through the long grass littered with bottles and cans to a shed.

"Look on the bright side, it could be worse." Jax trotted by and made herself comfortable in a small clearing in the grass.

"Yeah." Puck chuckled and cleared a space for Missy and the kittens.

The night was cold but everyone except for Ouji rested soundly. The sky was clear and all was silent. Ouji found it hard to sleep in such uncomfortable silence. After sleeping in the city to traveling on the train Ouji was use to the noise. Small cracks of the grass caused Ouji's ear to twitch, honing in on the sound. He felt uneasy, like someone or something was watching them. He jumped when he felt a warm breath on his neck, but when he turned there was no one there, only his sleeping friends. He watched the grass sway with sleepy eyes, but swore he saw a figure move in the darkness.

Senior wanted to get moving bright and early the next morning but Missy protested. She insisted that if she was going to visit a new place then they should explore first. After all, the forest wasn't going anywhere. They found a compromise and decided they would leave tomorrow morning, much to Puck's relief as his paws were tired and his stomach was empty.

The old town was the epicenter of business for the humans that worked in the lumber yard. Unlike the humans in the city, these ones moved a lot slower. There was no rush, no speeding metal cars, just folks passing by with no worry at all. Ouji set off to explore by himself. He was curious about the place and took Adrian along with him. According to Adrian, humans built all sorts of living dwellings. This one was called a town; it was like a city, but much smaller. Humans who lived in towns were friendlier and kind hearted. Ouji liked this town; it reminded him of Samantha, because of all the smiling happy faces. Walking through the town Ouji was mesmerized by the large hanging metal tubes that sang in the gentle breeze. They hung from almost every shop and together sounded like a chorus of chimes. It was marvelous how they twinkled and shined, he'd never seen anything like it.

"Adrian, what are those?" Ouji pointed to the tubes of metal hanging from a string.

The old mouse looked up and around until his eyes found what Ouji was focusing on. "Oh! I nearly forgot about those things. They're called wind singers; they sing when the breeze goes by." They both paused and listened as the breeze blew in from the mountain.

"They're beautiful." Ouji stood and listened.

"Yes indeed. You will find that everything in the forest has its own tune, you just have to stop and listen every once in a while."

Ouji smiled and nodded as he continued his journey through the town. He tried to stay out of the humans' eyesight as Puck warned, but it was hard with so many things to do and see. Ouji wanted to go into every shop and smell everything. Just off the main road was a large scrap yard filled with piles of old cars and junk. Adrian called this place a junkyard, a place where humans tossed out things they no longer needed anymore, but to Ouji it was a treasure trove of surprises. Ouji marveled at its overwhelming size. He walked through the uneven paths towards an old wooden shop with barrels of cans decorating on its sides. It looked abandoned, with its patched up roof and chipped paint. As he got closer he noticed that there was an old dog laying on the porch. Ouji froze immediately but the dog did not move. With caution Ouji approached, despite Adrian's protest. Ouji couldn't help but be a little curious as he walked closer. He had not met many dogs in his lifetime so he was very fascinated by them. He poked his paw just over the faded green porch. The old dog breathed out and opened one eye. Ouji snuck down and hid.

"No need to get jumpy." The old dog said with a scruffy voice as the hound yawned and stretched, waiting for the cat to reappear.

"I'm sorry to wake you." Ouji said in a small voice.

"Hmm." The hound grunted.

Ouji shrunk down lower, looking at Adrian who also was at a loss of what to do. "Um." Ouji poked his head just above the porch. "My name is Ouji."

The old hound lifted up one of his floppy ears. "Hmm, it's very nice to meet you Ouji. The name's Dodge."

Ouji smiled. He liked the way his name sounded when Dodge spoke. He hopped onto the porch with Adrian on his back. "And this is my friend Adrian."

Dodge nodded. "Nice to meet you too Adrian." The old hound raised the wrinkles on his brow and looked at the gray mouse perched on Ouji's back.

"The pleasure is mine." Adrian smiled as he twitched his long gray whiskers.

The old hound blinked in surprise when he noticed that Adrian was a mouse; he'd never seen a cat and a mouse be friendly with one another. He chuckled to himself and rose into a sitting position and coughed. He looked at the two animals before him. He couldn't remember the last time he had company, but he was pleased nevertheless and welcomed the newcomers.

"So what brings you to the little old town of Newberry?" the hound asked as his tail wagged softly on the porch.

"We're just passing through." Ouji said. "We're on our way to the forest."

The old hound gave the cat a skeptical look. "The forest? You don't say."

Ouji nodded. "We're headed to a place called Lion's Rock."

"Ohajidi?" the old hound mumbled.

"That's right!" Ouji stood in excitement; it was nice to hear that others knew of this place as well.

The old hound chuckled as he stretched again and lowered himself down onto his comfy bed on the porch. He hadn't heard the name Lion's Rock in such a long time. It was said to be a cat's paradise back in the old days. He remembered when he was young seeing the cats make the voyage. He never saw any of those cats again but he was sure they got to where they were going. Dodge himself hadn't been in the forest in a very long time, he missed hunting foxes with his master in the old days. He remembered the fresh taste of the water and crisp mountain air, all fond memories, but for a younger dog.

"Ouji, that's quite the interesting name you have there." Dodge spoke with his eyes nearly closed.

"Yes, it's dog for 'always be.'" The base of Ouji's tail shook as he remembered his dear friend, the one who had gave him his name.

Dodge nodded and smiled. It was very rare for a cat to have a dog name, let alone be so proud of it. Not many dogs knew their own tongue, many of his domesticated friends had forgotten their forest origin. For a cat to be gifted with such a special name, meant that he was destined for great things. "Well Ouji, I wish you and your friends luck."

"Thank you Dodge." Ouji bowed in respect.

Dodge allowed Ouji and Adrian to explore the junkyard. It was his master's place, filled with miles and miles of hidden treasures. Ouji was amazed looking at every pile, filled with things he had never seen before, exotic trinkets and knickknacks that with a little tail wiping shone like new. Ouji dug through the mounds of treasure, playing with tiny metal objects and discarded junk. It was quite entertaining for the young cat. He couldn't believe that humans actually threw this stuff out. There were cans, and mirrors, old pipes Ouji could crawl in, even old cars.

"Adrian, look at me I'm a person!" Ouji sat on the leather seats of an old 1967 Chevrolet Impala, with his paws on the leather steering wheel just like the people did. It was amazing that someone could actually make this thing move.

Adrian chuckled as he modeled in the chrome of an old rim. "I'd say, this is rather fun." Adrian chuckled at his distorted image.

Ouji hopped down from the car when he heard a noise. He turned his ear in the direction of the sound, but there was no one there.

"Dodge?" Ouji looked around.

He looked back at Adrian who was resting in the dirt. Ouji pawed him gently and motioned him to get on his back. Ouji walked cautiously towards where he heard the sound, but stopped midway. He looked to his left and then to his right but didn't see anyone down the dirt paths of the junkyard.

"Is there something the matter?" Adrian asked.

"I don't know." Ouji looked up at his friend.

A can bounced and tumbled down a pile of scrap next to them. It hit the ground and rolled out onto the middle of the path. Ouji looked at it but did not move. He sniffed the air but did not pick up the scent of anyone.

"That's odd," Ouji whispered.

Ouji walked slowly over to the can to investigate when he heard a low blood curdling growl. He looked up and saw a wild dog with gray and copper fur, with a crazed look in his eyes. He stood atop an old car, growling, teeth bare, with the fur sticking up on his back. Ouji hissed and turned tail and ran. This dog was not a friendly one. The dog howled and chased after him. Ouji dared not look back but prayed that Adrian held on tight. The dog quickly closed the gab between them and snapped his teeth at Ouji's tail. Ouji jumped high into the air and ran in zig zags to get away from the dog. He was terrified and had no idea where to go. He thought if he could make it back to the porch, he would be safe. The dog barked and growled as he chased after them through the junkyard. He was fast, but Ouji was faster thanks to his feline agility. Ouji made a sharp right around a large pile of pipes and sinks. He looked back and the dog was gone. Ouji sighed with relief and continued running but slowed down to catch his breath. Dust rained from the sky and Adrian screeched. The dog was suddenly right on top of them, running down a pile of metal scraps. Ouji hissed and ran but the dog pounced out in front of him, just barely missing Ouji and Adrian by inches. Ouji scratched and hissed at the dog before running back towards the entrance. Just around the other pile was the way he got in. He was almost there when the dog snagged his back legs with his paws, sending Ouji and Adrian rolling hard in the dirt. The dust cleared and Adrian was laying on the ground just feet away from Ouji. The dog had Ouji pinned under his paws. The dog howled, licking his lips. Ouji closed his eyes; he was done for sure. Without warning, the dog burst into a fit of laughter. Ouji opened one eye. He didn't understand what was so funny and looked over at Adrian, who was just as confused.

"That's enough!" Dodge said as he trotted over.

Ouji rushed to Adrian's side when Dodge appeared, wiggling out of the other dog's grip.

"What? I was just kidding." The once vicious dog had turned docile.

Dodge gave him a look. He did not appreciate the games he played.

"Aww, you're no fun, old timer." The dog stood and walked over to Ouji. The cat was immediately on guard, but the dog didn't show any signs of aggression. "You're fast for a cat." The dog stood before him, showing off the cream colored fur on his chest. Ouji looked at Dodge not sure what to do. He was still uneasy from the chase. "Where are my manners." The copper colored dog gave a toothy grin. "The name's Kaji."

Ouji glared. He did not trust him, but let his guard down just a bit when he saw how relaxed Dodge was around him.

Dodge shook his head. "Kaji."

"What?" Kaji smiled and shook the dirt from his fur. "I was just having a little fun."

Dodge ignored Kaji and walked over to Ouji and Adrian. "Are you hurt?"

Ouji shook his head. "I'm fine."

"Ignore Kaji, he seems to have forgotten his manners." The older dog scolded.

Kaji grinned. "Hey, no harm no foul," he joked.

Though Ouji had a hard time believing it at first, Kaji was actually a wild dog, like his wolf cousins. He chose to become a house dog and live with humans. Kaji and Dodge were both loyal working dogs that served their masters faithfully. While Dodge was raised from a puppy, Kaji was found by his master when he was only a year old. Folks thought he would be too wild to be a pet, but Kaji proved to be one of the best hunting dogs they had ever seen. He guarded the lands from wolves and bears and stuck by his master's side, protecting the pack, dog and human both. He was fiercely loyal, but still took pleasure in a good joke from time to time.

As night began to crawl in, Dodge invited Ouji and his friends to stay with him for the night. His masters who owned the junkyard were an older couple who often took in strays as they came and went. They were fed and given fresh water by the elderly couple, who seemed happy to have the company. Ouji and all his friends were very grateful for the invitation. It was nice to sleep in a home again. Ouji missed it more than he thought he would. He settled in next to a space heater while the others talked and ate. He enjoyed the waves of heat the machine produced and wished he could take it with him for the long winter ahead. In the dim light of the den Ouji's ears perked up when he heard someone approaching. Turning, he glared when he saw that it was Kaji.

"No hard feelings right?" Kaji grinned as he dropped a large ham bone at Ouji's side. It made a loud thud, causing the hair on Ouji's tail to puff out. "Ah, cheer up chap. It gets better; there's nothing to kill ya out here." Kaji laid down next to him and started to gnaw on his bone. "Say, you house cats traveled a long way to find a home." Kaji continued to chew.

"We're not looking for homes." Ouji turned his head away from the dog.

Kaji raised an eyebrow. "What? You want to live in the wild?" Kaji joked. When Ouji ignored him Kaji only laughed harder. "Eh, wild out here ain't so bad. Food's good. Humans are nice, pet or not."

Ouji rolled his eyes. He wanted Kaji to go away, but the dog looked pretty settled in. "If you must know," Ouji glared at the dog, who paid him no mind. "We're heading into the forest."

Kaji tilted his head. "The forest? Now why would you go and do a stupid thing like that?"

Ouji was surprised by his reaction, given Kaji's past. "Why not?"

Kaji chuckled. "Why not? Look around, kid. There's free food, shelter what else could you ask for?"

Ouji huffed. "Like you would understand."

Kaji laughed again. "Hey, if you want to go out into the woods and get yourself killed, that's your business." Ouji glared at Kaji again, but the dog wasn't joking around anymore. "The forest isn't a place for a house cat."

Ouji searched Kaji's eyes. "I can handle it," Ouji said with more force in his voice, but felt uneasy under Kaji's stare.

Kaji stood "Your funeral, but I would be careful who you trust your life to." Kaji grabbed his bone and joined Dodge in the living room.

Ouji watched Kaji leave. He was curious why someone who'd grown up in the forest would have such negative feelings towards it. He wanted to focus more on these thoughts but the warmth from the space heater lulled him to sleep.

In the morning, Senior was eager to leave, waking everyone up right before sunrise. They'd wasted enough time already. Dodge made sure they all ate before they started their long journey. Both dogs wished them luck; they'd both walked through the forest hundreds of times and knew the dangers that laid ahead. Dodge, who was worried about the group, suggested that Kaji go with them, but

Senior would hear nothing of it. The old cat knew where he was going and was certainly not going to take any help from a dog. They said their goodbyes and started down the dirt road again. Ouji watched Dodge and Kaji fade in the distance, Kaji's stern look reminding him of the words he said the night before. He tried not to let it bother him. He looked ahead and focused instead on Jax running and playing with the kittens. He had come so far. He was sure he was prepared for whatever the forest had in store for him.

Chapter Six

The town was in the far distance by the time the sun reached its high point in the sky. Senior, Bre, and Brett pushed forward, while Missy and Jax played with the kittens. Ouji hung back with Puck to keep him company, on the soft trail of pebbles and grass. Ouji couldn't believe he was here and was really extremely grateful to Puck for letting him tag along on this adventure. He felt like he was living the dream of the stories he heard as a kitten. He only wished he could have taken all his friends with him. He missed his city friends and he even missed Cheddar, but he was happy to at least have Adrian with him. He'd hoped this journey would reunite Adrian with his family in the forest. It was the least he could do after all the little mouse had done for him.

"A lot on your mind?" Puck glanced at his friend, whose eyes were as blank as paper.

Ouji jumped out of his daydream and looked at his friend. "Who me? Oh no." He tried to laugh it off.

Puck laughed harder. "Ah, you don't have to tell me if you don't want to." Puck chuckled. He stared in front of him, watching Missy play with her kittens. "See that? That's freedom, my friend." Ouji stared, trying to figure out what Puck meant. "Being with the folks you care about and going to the places you wanna go. Nothing in this world can beat it."

Ouji nodded. "Yeah." He watched Jax play with the kittens. He would go anywhere she went. She was his world now, stealing glances when he could. His eyes would dilate and his heart would race. It was an overwhelming feeling that made him nervous but also filled him with joy.

"Oh, I see got feelings for Jax huh?" Puck teased.

"Ah, no. Maybe." Ouji shied away.

"Ah, no complaints." Puck chuckled. "She's quite the cat."

"Yeah." Ouji looked back fondly at Jax.

They were coming up on a fork in the road and the group decided to take a quick break near a slow moving stream. In its crystal clear waters, much to Puck's delight were hundreds of tiny silver fish. As Puck watched, his stomach began to growl. The fish looked so tantalizing. Puck crouched down, his big orange butt high in the air and jumped in right into the stream, scaring most of them off in his sloppy attempt to hunt. Missy laughed and walked over to the stream to join him. She sat and waited patiently for a little fish to come within striking zone, easily nabbing up the first fish with her claws. Puck laughed, he was more amazed than jealous. He licked his lips as Missy let him have the first bite. He thanked her graciously, eagerly watching and learning from the talented mother. Ouji watched Bre and Bret hunt a distance away from the others while Jax fished. She turned around and rolled her eyes at Ouji. She shook her head. He would never learn to fish if he sat around daydreaming all the time. She took a fish and threw it at Ouji's face.

The tiny silver fish knocked Ouji awake as he wrinkled his nose and shook his head. "Hey? What the...?"

"You had that look on your face again." Jax walked over to him. She dropped another fish at his feet and giggled at Ouji's attempts to catch the flopping silver fish at his feet.

"It's nothing." They both knew he wasn't a very good liar. "I was just worried about Bre and Brett." Ouji sat next to his friend as Adrian munched on acorns next to him.

Jax sat next to him. "It's okay, it's how they've always been. I'm sure to an outsider it might look like they're giving you the cold shoulder, but they're just not really talkers."

Ouji nodded. He took a bite of his fish and gobbled it down. He shouldn't worry so much; after all he had only known the twins for a few weeks, but he couldn't help himself. He hadn't known many cats for too long, so it was hard for him to pick up on what was normal. Maybe that was just how some cats were; maybe some cats didn't need a lot of friends.

Jax looked up and chuckled. "So messy." Jax licked away a scrap of fish tail from the corner of Ouji's mouth. "There, all better."

The gesture made all his fur ruffle up, but as he watched her walk away, all his worries left with her. The group headed out soon after, and came to the fork in the road. There was a large wooden post in the middle with two brown signs; one with a picture of a square with teeth and trees, and the other with a number. Senior glanced back and forth as the group huddled behind him. He could feel their eyes on him, waiting for him to make a decision. Feeling rushed, he decided that they would take the route with trees, assuring them that this was the right way. Satisfied, no one questioned him and they followed him down the dirt path.

They walked for miles, down a lightly traveled path. They were surrounded by miles and miles of trees that stretched high into the sky. No one had ever seen trees this tall. They passed what felt like thousands, hopping over stumps and cleanly cut logs. The air was filled with freshly cut wood, soil, and leaves that covered the ground in beautiful vibrant fall colors. Ouji jumped onto a stump to catch a falling leaf. He caught it on his nose and held it there. Jax watched and laughed as the black cat balanced the leaf.

"Look! No paws!" Ouji laughed.

"Ouji you crazy- Ouji look out!" Jax screamed.

Ouji was startled and turned around, just in time to see a falling tree falling right for him. He dodged just in time but it seemed like the forest was falling all around them now. The cats ran as the sound of the tree cutters shook the earth below them. Missy, Puck, and Jax each grabbed a kitten while trying to dodge the cascade of falling trees.

"Quickly! To the edge!" Senior shouted as everyone ran for their lives.

"Hold on!" Ouji shouted to Adrian.

"Trust me! I have no intention of letting go!" Adrian held on tight to the scruff of Ouji's neck.

Ouji ran up a fallen tree behind his friends as the trees continued to fall. Machines rolled around them, deafening as they went, cutting and slicing trees. Ouji ran, as fast as he could, and up ahead he could see Senior and the twins were close to the forest edge. Safety was not far; Ouji focused in on that spot. A tree fell in his path but he bounced over off it. Through it he saw an opening and headed straight for it. It wasn't far now; he could see his friends, nearly to safety. He charged for the opening he saw, a gap between a pile of stumps and fallen trees. He was nearly through when he tripped and flew into the air, sending him and Adrian rolling into the dirt. Adrian landed safely in the leaf litter, but right into the path of another freshly cut tree. Ouji didn't even think; he ran right for his friend. The tree closed in.

"Ouji!" Jax froze mid step as she watched the tree hurtle towards him. She dared not look and shut her eyes.

Ouji didn't hear her, frozen in the wake of the falling tree.

"Stupid Cat!" Something knocked into Ouji and Adrian, pushing them out of the path of the tree.

Ouji landed hard on the ground, his heart pounding out of his chest.

"What are you standing around for? Run!" Kaji shouted at him.

Ouji grabbed Adrian and followed Kaji to safety.

"Head left!" Kaji shouted to the group as the machines made their way towards them.

He rounded everyone up; even Senior with all his stubbornness followed without complaint. Kaji ran at top speed. "This way!" he shouted and led the group to the edge of the lumber forest. They plunged into a ditch, rolling down the hill of fallen leaves and debris. Out of breath, the cats collapsed into the dirt. They were startled but everyone was okay.

"Kaji." Ouji turned to the dog in surprise. Kaji stood before him, breathing hard from exertion. He looked like the wild dog he once was, standing in the foreground of the trees.

"What were you trying to do? Get yourself killed?" Kaji barked.

"We...we didn't know." Ouji bowed down.

"That's right! You didn't!" Kaji growled. He saw the fear and worry in Ouji's eyes, but this was his path, his choice. Kaji composed himself. "Are you hurt?"

Ouji shook his head.

"Out there," Kaji turned and looked at the forest. "It's going to be ten times more dangerous than playing dodge with falling trees." Ouji froze and stared at the looming forest. "You think you can handle that?" Kaji asked.

Ouji was scared, terrified, but something about being in the face of danger made his resolve stronger. It was frightening, but his desire to see this through outweighed his fear. He nodded. "I can."

Kaji raised his brow and smiled. He licked away a few stray twigs from Ouji's long black fur and shook the dirt from his own body. "Has anyone ever told you you're a crazy cat?" Kaji joked.

Ouji smiled. "I guess you have to be a little crazy to want to live in a forest filled with danger."

Kaji laughed. "Yeah."

He didn't linger long, wishing his friends the best of luck as he left. Once back at the junkyard, Kaji rested on the porch with Dodge.

Howls carried in the wind, and Dodge raised his ear. Kaji smiled and listened. "Always be, huh." Kaji looked up at the full moon in the clear star-filled sky. "Good luck kid." He drifted back to sleep.

Chapter Seven

It took some time for the group to recover from their close encounter with the tree cutters. They all knew this journey was going to be dangerous, but the reality of such was just starting to set in. They looked to Senior for guidance knowing that the wise cat would lead them to safety, and just hoped the worse of it was over now that they had reached the forest.

The sunset as they ventured deep into the forest for the night. The thick brush would be plenty protection from the unknown dangers of the night and much safer than the outskirts of the lumber yard. As they traveled the echoing sounds from the lumber yard began to fade into a peaceful silence. Fall was in full swing here and looked nothing like the autumns from their hometowns. The ground was covered in a crunchy coat of red, yellow, orange, and brown.

Every tree was naked, stripped of their summer leaves making the bare branches look like roots in the sky. Ouji looked above him at a flock of migrating birds; to them, Ouji figured that he and his friends must look like ants on the ground. He wondered where they went this time of year, he thought to himself as he crossed a stream, the water so clear that he could see the pebbles of sand on the bottom. It was so scenic and surreal, how beautiful it was out here, Ouji couldn't imagine how anyone would want to live anywhere else. Senior said the path to paradise would be just where the mouth of the river begins. Ouji couldn't wait to see the river; he couldn't imagine how such tiny streams could evolve into such vast waters. To him it seemed impossible, but then again so did the idea of big cities and roaring trains. This was a new world and anything was possible.

The sunset on their first day in the forest and the group decided to settle next to the stream. Missy found the perfect spot in a hollow tree, a hole big enough for all of them to sleep to fend off the chill of the night, as it was much colder here. As night fell and the darkness set in, Ouji couldn't believe how dark it was. He struggled to see as the light fled from the forest floor. Even expert hunters Bre and Brett were having trouble seeing in the darkness; it was nothing like the street-lit city the cats were used to. The moon was covered by clouds, shedding only enough light to see a few feet ahead. They decided to hunt in pairs, Bre and Brett and Jax and Ouji, and they set off to find food, leaving the others behind. They were wary of the night, but they needed to find food and adjust to this new world.

"It sure is dark out here." Ouji shivered.

Jax nodded, though Ouji couldn't see. She was used to the dark. Her expert ears could single out sounds with ease, but it was hard to pinpoint sounds out here. They all seemed to bounce off the trees. She froze and looked behind her when she heard the sound of flapping wings; the noise encircled them then faded away, leaving no clue of its location.

"Hmm, it's going to be really hard to hunt at night." Jax said. "Let's head back, maybe we'll have better luck in the morning."

"Good idea." Ouji turned and followed.

Even though it was pitch black, Ouji's sense of smell could follow Jax. He noticed over time how much better his sense of smell had gotten, and wondered if in time his eyes would catch up too. A branch snapped and he stopped, looking up but only saw the silhouette of trees. He sniffed the air and his nostrils filled with scents he had no words for. It all smelled like earth mixed with leaves and animal droppings and water, impossible to tell what was important and what wasn't. He couldn't hunt like this with some many unknowns. He rushed to catch up with Jax and made a mental note to learn the name of every smell he came in contact with. He would get better at this; he would not fail.

Back at the campsite, Bre and Brett had had better luck. They had managed to hunt down a rabbit. Ouji cringed at the smell. He still didn't like to eat other animals, but what other choice did he have? He turned to Adrian, but the old gray mouse understood. This was the way of the forest, and the unbreakable cycle of life that benefited them all. It didn't seem to bother the mouse at all. Sometimes Ouji forgot that Adrian too came from this forest and he was sure the mouse had seen and lived through many things. He wondered how many obstacles the mouse had overcome. There must have been hundreds as Adrian made the journey alone from the forest to the neighborhoods, an amazing feat that even someone as brave as Senior could have made.

After dinner, Ouji settled in with Adrian and Jax for the night. He had a lot on his mind. He thought about how he was going to adapt to this new lifestyle, about Kaji and his words and the future of his own friends, about paradise and how it would be. He wondered about the cats that were running wild and free and a little part of him wondered if this was too good to be true. Jax purred as if to settle his mind and lull him back to sleep. A newly wildcat like him need not worry. For sleep was more important.

"Mom! Wake up! Wake up!" Uma pounced on her mother in the early hours of the morning.

Missy yawned and lifted her head. "What is it dear?"

"Look!" Serma shouted.

Uma joined her brother as they both stood on top of Puck. Missy turned her head and saw a herd of large four-legged creatures with huge bone-like horns. Missy pulled her children down off of Puck; she'd never seen anything like it. The others woke and were all on guard immediately.

"What are those grandfather?" Bre stared ahead, not afraid but curious as her eyes sized up the creatures.

"Ah, they're..." Senior stuttered as he looked at the tan and white hooved creatures.

"They're deer." Adrian yawned. Everyone turned to the little gray mouse. "White-tailed deer." The little mouse smiled.

Senior huffed. "White-tailed deer, just what I was going to say," the older cat huffed.

Missy turned to Adrian. "Are they dangerous?"

"Oh heavens no, but I wouldn't get in their way." Adrian wrinkled his nose and shook his whiskers.

Serma jumped onto Puck's head. "Can we eat 'em?"

Adrian chuckled. "You'll need to be a little bit bigger to take down a full-sized deer."

Ouji turned to his friend. "What kind of creature could eat something that big?"

Adrian paused. "Hmm, maybe a bear or a wolf. I wouldn't put it past a bobcat to take down a small fawn."

Puck sat in shock. "Golly, they must be really big."

Adrian nodded. "Wolves and bears are some of the fiercest creatures in the forest, but they are nothing compared to the stealth and speed of the great horned owl." Adrian shuddered.

Jax turned and watched the majestic creatures pick through the leaves. "Wow."

With the snap of a twig, all the deer froze. The largest buck turned and listened and led the herd away. The cats watched them leave in amazement and wonder over the creatures that stood as tall as man.

Serma turned to his mother. "Momma, when I grow up I'm gonna get big and strong so I can hunt a deer!" Serma puffed out his chest.

"Yeah right!" Uma jumped on his back and the two of them rolled around in the dirt.

Missy watched her kittens play, and while she urged Tama to join in, the kitten was still too scared to leave the safety of his mother.

"I'm going out to find food; play nice with your brother and sister." Missy stood, despite Tama's protest, and nodded to Puck to watch the children.

"Alright gang." Puck stood and stretched. "How about a game of hide and seek?"

The kittens turned to the big orange tabby and smiled. Ouji and Jax chuckled from the side as they watched Puck hide his eyes, tail up and count for the kittens.

"Did you play many games when you were a kitten?" Jax asked.

"I did, but nothing as fun as that." Ouji thought of all the times he played chase the tail with his siblings. "I mean, I never had the chance to live in a place big enough to run around like this."

"You grew up in a home right?"

Ouji nodded. "And before that, a shelter."

Jax stared at him in disbelief. She couldn't imagine the horrors of growing up in a pound. "Oh that must have been horrible." She frowned.

"It wasn't so bad." Ouji stared at the playful kittens. "I had my family." He frowned.

"And where are they now?"

"I don't know." Ouji turned to look at her.

Jax lifted her paw and placed it on top of his. "I'm sure they wound up in homes just like you." She smiled. Ouji found comfort in her big green eyes and nodded. He wanted to believe that too.

Senior sat the farthest away glaring at the group. He wanted to get moving but everyone insisted they take another break. He huffed as he shook the leaf litter from his dark smoky fur. He was so close to paradise, he could practically taste it. He was sure following the river's path would lead him to his destiny, there he would find his peace and become ruler of paradise. He reveled in the idea for a bit longer before Bre returned with his food.

"Where is your brother?" Senior said coldly.

"He is on his way, grandfather." Bre laid the food at her grandfather's paws.

Senior grunted as he took the food without thanks. "I can tell which one of you is the most valuable to me." He gobbled down the food with no intention of sharing.

"Brett is strong and fast, grandfather, and he will always be loyal to you."

Senior hissed. "Must be his father's genes dirtying up the bloodline. In you, my dear granddaughter, I can see a future." Senior purred.

She looked shyly away from her grandfather's compliments.

Senior grinned. "Here, eat up. You'll need your strength."

"Grandfather I couldn't."

"Nonsense, I won't have my strongest hunter starve and wither away before my old eyes." He sat next to her. She smiled and gladly took the offering.

Bre and Brett were the only other surviving members from Senior's family line. He had had brothers and sisters but they had long since passed. Senior himself had only taken one mate in his lifetime, an abandoned house cat named Alice, whose beauty rivaled none. Together they had one litter before she was taken away by the catchers. In that litter Senior had three kittens, two daughters, Ashma and Ashita, and one son named Arben, who died in his first winter. Senior loved his daughters very much and was very protective of them, but life was hard growing up in the city. Back in those days the catchers patrolled the streets like dogs, picking up and trapping any stray they could find. Senior warned his daughters about the dangers of the city but younger cats are hard headed and his daughters were no exception. He lost Ashita on a cold rainy night, when a careless human ran her over. His heart broke as he was left with only one daughter and his grief led him to be very hard on her and Ashma grew up to be one of the toughest cats in the city.

On one cool fall evening Ashma met a tomcat named Timkey. He was smart and funny and made her laugh. He broke down her cold exterior and to Senior that made her weak. Senior hated that cat, and to that day he blamed him for his daughter's death. He watched from the background as his daughter grew up and moved farther and farther away from him. He let her go, as he knew she loved him. It was hard, but the right thing to do. He re-entered her life when he heard the news that Ashma had given birth to her first litter of kittens. She had five tiny little kittens and Senior was very proud. He stayed with her and protected her but his coldness drove a wedge between her and Timkey, who grew jealous. Not wanting to upset his daughter, he left, but promised to visit every night of the full moon. She was delighted, but he was never given the chance to keep his promise.

On the second night she'd fallen ill in the cold winter air. The box Timkey had raised his family in was made of cardboard and it had gotten wet and broken down. In a last ditch effort to save his family, Timkey left to find better shelter, but when he returned a group of humans were raiding his box and taking Ashma and her kittens away. He ran to her and fought the humans tooth and claw, but his heart broke when he saw Ashma's lifeless body in their arms. He wailed and ran from the scene; there was nothing more that he could do.

On the first full moon Senior returned to visit his daughter as promised. He went to the spot his daughter and Timkey had made their home, but found no one. Worried for his daughter and grandchildren, he ran all around the city in search of them. When he got to the last safe house he ran into an old friend who had seen the events the night before. He said that in Timkey's absence, humans had taken Ashma and her kittens away. Senior, stricken with grief and anger, asked where Timkey had went, but was told that the coward had run away and hasn't been heard from since. Senior broke down. He'd lost everything in one night; all his joy had been sucked away.

But, his friend told him, the humans had missed two. They were the smallest kittens and had been easily overlooked because of their dark fur. His friend had found them under the cardboard. Senior was overjoyed. He took the kittens and raised them under an iron fist. He thought them how to hunt and fight and survive and never let them out of his sight.

The days were getting shorter and the nights longer, but the group continued on. Determined to beat the winter freeze, they relied on Senior's stories of paradise to carry them through the bitter cold. They looked forward to the endless food and the crystal clear waters of Lion's Rock. Even Senior seemed like he was in a better mood. Adrian taught Ouji how to pick out which berries and nuts were safe to eat and taught him how to keep an ear out for predators. Adrian warned that there were many eyes and ears in the forest and it was important to always be on guard. Ouji took his warnings to heart. He relied heavily on the knowledge Adrian passed on and learned everything he could to become a better wildcat.

As each day passed Missy and Puck enjoyed watching the kittens grow. They were getting bigger and stronger from the miles of walking and climbing. Missy's only wish was that Tama would come out of his shell. She pushed him along every time his siblings went out to play, because she knew that one day she would not be here to protect him.

It was mid-day and the group decided to take a break. Everyone was exhausted and though Senior wouldn't admit it, he was just as tired as the rest of the group. They once again camped next to the stream, like they had every night since they started. They would pick up again tomorrow bright and early, but for now they would rest up and re-charge for the day.

Serma, full of energy, ran around camp chasing leaves, insects, and anything else that fell in front of him. He whizzed past his sister and up the trunk of a tree. He was a good climber now and was never afraid to scale the trees. Uma joined him, trying to see who could climb the highest. Tama watched cautiously from the safety of the ground.

"Come on Tama, what are you scared of?" Serma asked as he and Uma sat perched atop the lowest branch on the tree.

Tama backed away and shook his head.

"How you gonna survive if you can't even climb a tree?" Serma ran to the edge of the branch and stared down at his brother.

"I-I won't need to." Tama shouted.

"Yeah, well what if there's food's up here?" Serma retorted.

"First one to the top gets the first milk." Uma said as she took off up the tree.

"Aw! No fair! No head starts!" Serma chased after his sister.

Tama watched his brother and sister ascend the tree. They were always the first to try everything, brave and fearless and everything Tama was not. He was jealous; he wanted to be brave like them, but the world was a scary place. He felt like he would never be brave like them and he would always be a scaredy cat. Tama sat at the base of the tree and waited for the two of them to come down, when he heard a rustle in the leaves next to him. He stood and turned, ready to run away at the first sign of danger. When a tiny marbled salamander scurried onto a rock, Tama froze and watched the creature. It stopped when it saw him, then ran away under the leaves. Tama sighed in relief. He sat again at the base of the tree and waited, but after a while he became bored. He wished his siblings would play somewhere safe but they always went to the extreme. Tama decided he would make his own fun. Why did he always have to follow them? If they wanted to get eaten or fall out of a tree they could go right ahead, but he wasn't going to take that chance.

He walked a little, then looked back to make sure he wasn't too far, then walked a little further. He came to a small stream that broke from the river. He liked to watch the little fish and water insects swim in the currents. He pretended that he was a brave hunter and pawed at the tiny creatures. He played and dipped his paws in the cold water. He jumped in when he felt comfortable and splashed and played, making his own fun.

"What are you doing?" Serma looked down at him.

Tama froze and stared at his brother and sister, unsure when they had appeared. "N-Nothing."

"Yeah right, looks like fun." Serma ran down next to his brother. "How do you play?" Uma followed him.

Tama looked around nervously. "It's not really a game, but you just kind of chase the fish," he said shyly.

"Chase the fish?" Serma perked up his ears. "Sounds like fun!" He jumped in, making a big splash.

"Let me try! Let me try!" Uma jumped in too.

Tama watched his brother and sister play, surprised that they were actually having fun. He wanted to join them but he shied away.

"Where you going Tama?" Serma looked at his brother.

Tama froze. He didn't know what to say. Both of them were looking at him and not just to tease him, they were looking to him for direction. This was Tama's game and it wasn't fun without him.

"No-no where," Tama said softly. He held his breath and ran towards the stream and pounced into the water. He actually caught a fish under his paw. He looked up and saw both Serma and Uma staring at him.

"Nice one Tama!" Uma shouted.

"I wanna try! I wanna try!" Serma splashed and played.

The children played for hours until their mother called them in for dinner. She groomed them relentlessly and fussed at Puck for not watching them more carefully, but she was happy that her little Tama was coming out of his shell. That night the group was lucky; Bre, Brett, and Jax managed to catch a few fish. It was the perfect end to a restful day.

Night came quickly. The group nestled in close to the river banks. The night was silent. Adrian slept in the dark fluffy fur of Ouji's back. He tossed and turned trying to find a comfortable position, but he couldn't. He woke and stared into the night sky. It was so clear you could see every star in the sky, something the old mouse had missed. He sighed and finally gave up trying to fall back to sleep. He looked around in envy of all his sleeping friends, but there was no use dwelling on something he would not find. Adrian decided he would take a quick night stroll. He stood on his hind legs and sniffed the air, standing still and listening for any sounds. When it was clear he ran off into the night. He ducked inside of bushes and ran through areas of thick brush. Just a few feet away was a very large spider, and he smiled, licking his lips. He rarely had the chance to eat insects, but when he did find one he liked, he made sure to catch it. He paused and listened before making his move. He pounced on it and ate it in the safety of the thick brush. It was a tasty mid-night snack, one he was happy to finally taste again. His ear twitched, and he looked up, hearing the sound of fluttering wings. He froze. He was all too familiar with that sound and hid deep in the bushes. There was a swooping sound just over him and he heard the squeal of another mouse. Adrian gulped, but stayed hidden. When he heard another squeal he wondered if the owl had dropped the mouse, and sure enough, he heard the sound of running paws. He was terrified but against his better judgment he poked his head out from under the bush and running towards him he could see another deer mouse. Adrian had to think fast. If he helped the other mouse the owl would surely get them both, but he couldn't stand to see another one of his kind hunted down by an owl. He shook his head and gathered up all the courage he had to shout to the other mouse.

"Over here!" He shouted and hoped the other mouse heard.

The tiny gray and brown mouse heard and sped in the direction of the thick brush. Both mice froze and listened for the owl; they knew all too well that owls were strong hunters at night and so more than likely they would not be able to move until sun up. Adrian looked at the other mouse, and even in the cover of the darkness he could tell she was a young mouse. He worried for his new friend, but they could not speak. The two of them sat in silence until the sun rose the next day.

Adrian walked the young mouse back to the area where his friends were sleeping. It was safe now to travel home but the younger mouse was tired and scared after the events of the night and would not leave his side.

"Thank-thank you for saving me," the young mouse said quietly.

"Not a problem my dear." Adrian said to the younger mouse.

Adrian hoped that his friends would not be upset that he brought another creature along with him on their trip, but he could not leave her out there all alone. He looked back and noticed that she seemed uneasy. She looked behind her and over her shoulders a lot, and he could tell that she did not venture out during the day often.

"What is your name dearie?" he asked.

"Bettina."

"Bettina? Oh, what a beautiful name. Well Bettina, my name is Adrian."

She smiled a little. "Well it is very nice to meet you Adrian."

"The pleasure is mine." Adrian chuckled. "And just like you I was born and raised in this forest."

"Then why have I never seen you around?" She walked beside him.

"I've been away."

"Away?"

Adrian nodded. "Yes, past the city into human territory."

She gasped. "Past the city!" She cringed at the idea. Young mice were taught to never leave the forest. "How did you survive?"

"Well, it wasn't easy." Adrian closed his eyes and thought fondly of his family. "When I was a child I always had a nose for adventure. My mother saw it and she knew I would not be a mouse to stay around in the forest. My father worked hard to bring us fresh fruits and seeds, but he was terribly afraid of leaving the forest. When I was old enough I was allowed to leave the nest and that was the day I knew."

"Knew what?" Bettina asked.

Adrian turned to her and smiled. "That's the day I knew that I was destined for a life of adventure." The old gray mouse chuckled as the younger mouse stared in amazement.

They traveled quickly to the resting group. It was not far away but they still traveled cautiously. The forest at any time of the day was unsafe for little deer mice. As Adrian got closer he could hear Ouji calling his name.

"This way!" Adrian led Bettina.

"Adrian!" Ouji shouted. He was worried about his friend; it was unlike him to wander off in the middle of the night. "Adrian!"

Adrian and Bettina crossed under a decaying log and saw Ouji sniffing and turning over leaves.

Bettina froze when she saw the cat. "Bobcat!" She squealed and ran and hid.

Ouji turned around.

"Bettina!" Adrian shouted.

"Adrian, there you are." Ouji greeted his friend fondly, purring and rubbing against him "I was so worried."

"I am sorry that I worried you." Adrian hugged his friend.

This confused Bettina. She'd never known any bobcat to be so friendly, but she'd also never seen any bobcat with long black fur.

Adrian turned towards the bushes. "Ouji, I'd like you to meet my new friend. Bettina, you can come out. It's safe I promise, Ouji wouldn't hurt a fly."

Bettina was hesitant at first, but after she saw how calm Adrian was around Ouji she walked slowly out from the bushes.

Ouji perked up his ears and smiled. "Nice to meet you." He stepped forward, and Bettina stepped back.

"It's okay Bettina, he truly is friendly. He's the one who has been so kind to escort me home."

Bettina didn't say a word to Ouji but nodded and approached slowly. Adrian smiled and hopped onto Ouji's back. She looked up, unsure if she should follow suit. Adrian offered his paw and Ouji carried them both back to camp.

"So Bettina, are you a forest mouse too?" Ouji tilted his head.

"Y-yes sir I am." She said shyly.

"That's amazing, it must have been nice to grow up in a place like this." Ouji smiled.

She turned away.

Adrian noticed the sadness in her eyes. "Say Bettina, you weren't alone last night were you?"

She shook her head. "I-I was with my uncle."

"I see." Adrian frowned, lowering his eyes to the ground. "Ouji." He turned to his friend.

"Yes?"

"Could I ask you a favor?"

"Sure, anything you like." The fluffy cat smiled.

"I want to make sure Bettina gets home safely. I'm sure her mother must be worried sick." Adrian looked at the younger mouse.

"Of course!" Ouji picked up the pace towards the camp groups. "Let me just let the rest of the group know."

"The rest?" Bettina said with a little worry in her voice.

"Oh don't worry, everyone is super nice," Ouji reassured her.

They passed a low laying row of bushes that was right before the camp site. Jax was the first to greet Ouji. She was happy Ouji found his friend. Bettina was very scared at first but when she looked at the company around her and noticed everyone purring and smiling she felt much better.

"Who's your little friend?" Jax asked.

"Jax, gang, this is Bettina. I've agreed to help get her home," Ouji announced.

Senior snarled. "Might I remind you, we are on a very tight schedule!"

"Oh come on, Senior," Puck joked. "It's not like paradise is going anywhere."

The rest of the group agreed.

"It shouldn't take long." Adrian raised his head.

Senior glared at the little mouse.

"Just over the creek a ways down. We should be there and back in under a day," Adrian said pointing.

Missy purred. "That's doesn't sound too bad. I could use another break."

Puck smiled. "Say, why don't you and Jax go and we'll wait for you here."

Ouji nodded. "Thank you."

Senior grumbled but he couldn't leave without the others; no one would agree to that. "Be back by sundown!"

Ouji nodded. "Thank you Senior. Ready Jax?"

The gray and black tabby nodded. "Lead the way."

Adrian let Bettina lead the way. He wondered if she came from the same tribe as he did. The path seemed so familiar to him. He remembered running the old paths with his brothers and sisters. It would bring him so much joy if he could see them again. Bettina sat atop Ouji's head and whispered and pointed, leading the group to the mice's secret nesting grounds. She wouldn't lead them all the way but just far enough that she could walk.

"When we get there, you bobcats can't come in. The others would be scared."

"Bobcats?" Ouji asked.

"Yeah, it's what you are right?" Bettina looked at the two cats.

"Bobcat?" Ouji repeated, looking at Jax who was just as confused.

"Oh! I forgot about bobcats." Adrian shook his head. "Bettina my dear, these are pet cats."

"Pet cats?" Jax hissed.

"I mean, cats who are used to living around humans. Bobcats are forest cats."

"Wildcats?" Ouji asked.

"Yes." Adrian stated.

"Wow, I'd love to meet them." Ouji perked up his ears.

"Oh heavens no, Ouji. Bobcats are nothing like the cats who live in the city and neighborhoods. They're fierce and merciless creatures. They live closer towards the mountains and only venture down during the winter when food is scarce. I wouldn't wish an encounter with a bobcat on anyone," Adrian warned.

Ouji nodded, wondering what they looked like. He was interested now. They sounded pretty scary the way Adrian described them, but he wasn't sure if that was just the cautious mouse in him talking or if what he was really saying was true. Either way Ouji wanted to meet these wildcats, despite Adrian's warnings.

"Through there!" Bettina led them.

Ouji walked through the thick brush to a small clearing where a tree had fallen. It was a small patch of grass growing in the light from the hole in the canopy.

"We can walk from here." Bettina jumped off.

"Alright." Ouji settled down for a quick nap. "Adrian I'll be waiting when you get back.

Adrian nodded and thanked both Ouji and Jax for helping him get Bettina home safely.

"Follow me." Bettina smiled and the two disappeared into the sea of bushes.

Bettina led Adrian through the maze of bushes and leaf litter. The farther they moved the more he felt at home. It wasn't until he entered the nesting grounds that he realized where he was. It had been so long, it was like looking at the nest for the first time. Adrian froze as he watched the mice scurry under the protection of the prickly bushes.

Bettina stopped and looked back. "Mr. Adrian?"

"I'm, I'm home." Adrian's face lit up as his heart swelled with emotion.

Bettina smiled. "This way, I'd like you to meet someone."

"Of course." Adrian nodded.

He followed behind Bettina. They passed many mice, none that he recognized but it was still nice being surrounded by his own kind. There were lots of stares as the two walked over to a mound.

"Mother?" Bettina called out.

"Bettina!" There was a rustle in the grass and out appeared a larger tan mouse. "Bettina!" She ran to her daughter. "I was so worried about you!" She hugged Bettina so tight that she thought she would be squished. "Where's your Uncle?" The mother mouse looked around.

Bettina lowered her head.

"Oh no." The mother mouse gasped and placed a paw on her daughter's shoulder. She looked up and that's when she saw Adrian standing quietly at the foot of the nest. "I'm sorry, but have we met?"

"Oh no." Adrian chuckled. "I'm just visiting."

"Mother, this is Adrian. He saved me and brought me back home." Bettina smiled.

The mother smiled, and rushed over to Adrian to thank him. She offered him fresh food and place to stay for the night.

"Thank you." Adrian rubbed his paws together.

The mother mouse nodded and led Bettina back into the nest. "You coming?" she asked.

"In a minute, I would just like to check on something first."

"Take your time," the mother mouse said.

Adrian nodded and wandered off around the nesting ground, letting his memories guide him home. He made his way through the market place where there were mice trading all kinds of goods. He stopped to smell the freshly picked spider legs and forest seeds. He inhaled the aroma, which brought back so many childhood memories. He walked down the grassy lane, spotted with yellow-green shoots. He stopped to touch the fresh grass. He smiled and waved to passing mice and their pups. He turned at the smooth roots, that had now grown into large mature roots that formed a canopy tunnel down to his old nest. When he reached the end of the path he stopped. His home, it was still there. He scurried down, calling for his mother and father as he ran.

"Anyone home?" He stood and waited, but heard nothing. He sighed, but didn't give up hope. "Hello?"

"Who's there?" shouted two little voices.

"My name is Adrian," Adrian responded nervously.

"Uncle Adrian?" said the first voice, a young girl's voice.

A little head popped up from the rim of the nest. The tiny boy gasped. "He's alive. He's alive!" The little boy jumped around.

"Quick! Go tell Oma!" The little girl shouted and pointed.

Adrian stared at the two. His brain had frozen on the word uncle. Soon the rim of the nest was filled with mice. Adrian nearly fainted when he saw his entire family standing before him; all his brothers and sisters were alive. He was over joyed.

"Mother! Father! Cassandra! Daniel! Georgina! Helga! Ilsa! Eckart! Filibert!" Adrian shouted.

Each family member was delighted to see their long lost family member. They all ran to him and tackled him. They pulled him into the nest where each brother and sister was eager to catch him up on all that he had missed. All of his sisters had settled happily with their mates and had children of their own and his brothers as well. They had made this nest the family home, and cared for their mother and father there. They weren't upset that he had run off, just happy to see him alive and well. He shared his stories with his family well into the night and even told them how he saved a young mouse. The sun had set and Adrian had completely forgotten he needed to get back to Ouji to go to Lion's Rock. He turned to his family. It would not only break their heart to leave, but it would break his as well.

"Is something the matter?" his mother asked.

"No mother sorry to worry you, I'm fine." Adrian lied.

"Oh poppycock, I can see right through you Adrian." She laid a paw on her son's back. "I am so happy to have you home. We've missed you so much." She smiled.

It broke his heart even more. He wanted so much to stay, but he couldn't abandon his friends.

"Adrian."

"Yes mother."

"I've gotten to see you one last time, but I know your heart lies beyond these forest. If you need to go, I won't stop you."

Adrian looked at his mother, sadness welling up in his heart. He nodded, and left the nest quickly, running for the exit. Outside, Adrian found Ouji and Jax waiting patiently talking where he left them.

"Ouji!" Adrian shouted, out of breath.

"Adrian! I was worried sick, how's Bettina? Did she get home safe?" he asked.

Adrian nodded. "Ouji I found it."

Ouji looked at him. "Found what?"

"My home." Adrian smiled ear to ear.

Ouji's face lit up, and even Jax was happy to hear the news.

"That's wonderful Adrian!" Ouji purred and licked his friend.

"And I was wondering." Adrian lowered his voice. "Would it be alright with you, if I stayed?"

Ouji paused, and it worried Adrian. They had been through so much together; he didn't want to leave his friend, but his heart was where his family was, and to him, this was home. "Of course Adrian," Ouji said calmly, lowering himself to the mouse's eye level.

Adrian clasped his hands together. "Thank you Ouji! Thank you so much!" Adrian hugged his best friend, trying hard not to break down.

"I'm going to miss you." Ouji purred biting back the sorrow of losing his friend.

"Oh it won't be long, I promise." Adrian replied.

"Take care." Ouji stood and watched his friend scurry away.

Adrian turned and smiled one last time, shaking his whiskers. He nodded and turned and ran into the sea of bushes disappearing from Ouji's sight for the last time. Jax purred next to Ouji, who didn't try to hide his sadness. In the end, he was happy that he was able to help Adrian get home.

"You ready?" Jax stood beside him.

He nodded and followed Jax back to camp. Now all that was left was for him to find himself a place he could call home.

Chapter Eight

Their day started bright and early, just as the sun peeked over the horizon. Senior was very angry that Ouji and Jax returned so late last night, but no one had any intentions of traveling after sunset. It was dangerous and even Senior knew that, but still his impatience grew. He didn't have any time to waste and all the breaks and stops were driving him mad. If he didn't get to paradise soon he swore he would lose his mind. The group marched on following the river until it was about thirty to forty feet wide. It was all white water the closer they got to the mountains. They traveled quickly that day to make up for the past two days of breaks and no one complained as Senior pushed the group forward. Up in the front near Senior and the twins, Missy's kittens were laughing and playing. Tama was getting braver by the day and now began to follow when his brother and sister went off to play. Missy watched her kittens continue to grow, and it warmed her heart seeing her children adapt to their new home.

Uma sighed and shook the leaf litter from her paws. "I wonder when we'll get there," Uma complained.

"Hey!" Serma looked at his brother and sister. "I bet we'll get there by tomorrow!"

Tama ran behind them. "I don't know you guys, I don't see any mounds of food anywhere."

"That's cause Uncle Puck ate it all!" Serma snickered, and his siblings laughed along with him.

They didn't really care how long it took; they were having fun running and playing on the soft forest floor. There were so many things to do and best of all no catchers to nab them or metal machines to squish them. They lived without a care in the world and even Tama was starting to warm up to the place.

The group walked close to the river's edge, where the water was moving fast. Ouji hoped they wouldn't have to cross it. The water was cold and the current was strong it would be impossible to swim across. He couldn't believe this huge river turned into all those tiny streams they crossed at the start of their journey. He was truly amazed. The sun reached its highest point and the group settled down for a quick break. They rested in a sunny spot while the twins hunted for food. Ouji took the time to take a quick nap, while Jax went off for a drink of water. The kittens, full of energy, snuck off to play in the wild grass. It was long and grew high, so it was the perfect place for a game of hide and seek. The three chased each other through the grass all the way down to the river's edge. Serma looked down at the rushing water. There was a large overturned tree that fell and made the perfect bridge midway through the river. Serma's eyes lit up when he saw the stump.

"Hey, I double, no triple dare you to walk to the end of that tree to that rock over there." Serma turned his head towards the middle of the river where the tree had landed on a large algae covered rock.

Uma and Tama looked at the tree with worry.

"You're crazy," Uma said, turning her nose away.

"What are you, scared?" Serma teased as he ran closer to the tree to get a better look. His eyes glistened as he watched the white water rush below.

Uma huffed. "I'm not scared." Uma turned and watched her brother wiggle his tail near the water's edge.

The two kittens looked at Tama. "Wha-what?"

"You comin'?" Serma looked back at his brother.

Tama was terrified, but he didn't want to seem like a baby in front of his siblings, now that he had made so much progress. The old Tama would have ran and hid next to mom, but he didn't want to be that scared little kitten anymore. He nodded and all three of the kittens stood at the base of the tree stump.

"First one to the rock and back gets the best teat!" Serma shouted and grinned. "Alright! Ready? One... Two..." With that, Serma took off.

"Hey!" Uma hissed and chased after her cheating brother.

Tama followed behind slowly. He didn't want to look down but as he picked up pace he started to enjoy himself. Serma was in the lead and nearly to the end of the tree right as Uma was closing the gap.

"Gottcha!" Uma lunged high and jumped right onto Serma's back.

The two slid across the moss covered log and nearly felt off. Serma was able to dig his claws into the wood just in time to stop him and his sister from falling. Tama, however who was running at top speed, didn't notice that Uma and Serma had stopped right in the middle of the log. He couldn't stop in time and slammed into his brother and sister, causing Serma to slip off the log. Uma was quick to grab him by the scruff, but he was too heavy. Tama ran to help, but he couldn't lift both his brother and sister as his grip began to give way and all three of them fell into the freezing rapids below.

Missy was napping quietly when she heard the sounds of her kittens' cry. She was immediately on her feet. She called for them and when she heard no answer she ran towards the sounds. Her fine-tuned mother ears led her right to them. Puck and Ouji followed after they heard Missy scream.

"Missy! What's the matter?" Puck shouted.

"It's the kittens! They've fallen into the river!" she shouted as she ran along side them. "Hang on dears!"

"Mama!" Uma cried as her tiny head dipped under the fast moving rapids.

Missy, Puck and Ouji ran alongside the river. It was so wide, there was no way they could jump in. Missy ran down the steep river bank and kept alongside her kittens. Puck followed as Ouji ran above them to get a better took ahead.

"Puck! There's a tiny dip just ahead! It's dammed off!" Ouji shouted.

"I'm on it!" Puck shouted. "Missy! Tell the kittens to swim towards you! There's a dam up ahead, we can catch them there!"

Missy nodded and called her kittens towards her. Ouji and Puck ran as fast as they could to the dam to try and fish the kittens out. Missy shouted to her little kittens to swim towards her. The kittens struggled to swim; the water was moving too fast but they pumped their legs towards their mother as hard as they could. Ouji and Puck were now in position; they watched the water for the kittens, ready to grab them at a moment's notice. Tama, who was a surprisingly good swimmer managed to make it in the direction of the dam; Uma paddled hopelessly in the fast moving rapids. Missy grew worried when she could no longer see Serma. She called for him as the other two kittens made it in the direction of the dam.

"Serma! Serma!" Missy shouted and right as she shouted a little black head popped up above the rapids.

"Mama!" Serma shouted, trying to breathe above the fast moving water.

"Serma!" Missy shouted to her son.

"I see them!" Puck shouted. "Ready!" He shouted to Ouji, who nodded.

The two cats braced themselves to pull the two kittens from the water. Puck grabbed Uma who just missed the dam and Ouji grabbed Tama. They threw them to the banks and watched the waters for Serma. Missy ran alongside the waters, past Puck and Ouji. The boys looked at each other and then at the waters. They could see little Serma barely keeping his head above water.

"Ouji! Stay with the kittens!" Puck shouted.

Puck took off faster than he had ever ran in his life. He ran past Missy and dove into the cold waters. He was bigger and was able to navigate the waters much better. He swam with all his might to reach the drowning kitten. Missy followed them on the shoreline watching in fear as her friend risked his life to save her son. Puck pushed through the rapidly moving water and reached Serma just in time. He grabbed the tiny kitten by his scruff and swam against to the current toward the bank. Missy gasped when she saw Puck had grabbed him, and she picked up the pace, racing onto a set of rocks that ran into the middle of the river.

"Puck! This way!" she shouted.

Puck couldn't hear her, but he could see where she was standing. He swam towards to the rocks. It was very hard to fight the current and the tiny ebbs and dips sucked him under the water many times, but never once did he let go. He swam hard and was able to push himself up against the rocks under the water. Missy saw them and prepared herself. Puck could tell by how fast he was coming in that if Missy tried to grab them both she would surely fall in too. When he reached the rocks, he braced his back paws against the rocks. His right back paw slipped and got caught between two rocks. He growled but didn't let go of Serma. Missy ran right for him and scooped up Serma with her mouth and tossed him to the safety of the banks. She didn't have time to check him over as she tried to lift Puck out of the water too. She didn't realize his paw was stuck, but she tried anyways. Puck squirmed and yanked his paw free and Missy pulled him up.

"Serma!" She rushed to her son, who was not breathing. "Serma!" She licked his nose.

He coughed and looked up at his mother. "Mama."

"Oh Serma! Don't you ever do that to me again!" she scolded.

Puck sighed in relief and stood. He had a little limp, but nothing was broken. Missy let Serma ride on her back as she helped Puck back to the river bank, where Ouji, Uma, and Tama were waiting for them.

"Puck! Missy!" Ouji called out to his friends.

"Hey kiddo." Puck greeted his friend. His back paw was hurting more than he let on, and he collapsed at Ouji's paws.

"Puck!" Missy rushed to him to check on his paw.

"Oh it's nothing," he reassured her. "I've had plenty worse. Let's head back."

Ouji nodded. He and Missy carried the tired kittens on their backs as they helped Puck get back the resting site. Senior was not happy when he saw the group; he had grown tired of their constant breaks, but Missy was not having any of his sass today. She gave him one look and put him in his place. They would be camping where Missy said tonight.

Jax returned with a rabbit later that day. She was worried that she had been out for too long but everyone seemed like they were in no rush to her relief. She shared her kill with the group and sat next to Ouji who was setting alone staring off into the distance.

"Everything okay?" Jax asked.

Ouji sat, deep in thought. "Life is short Jax."

Jax laughed lightly. "Yeah-"

"Jax, I love you." Ouji blurted out, as his eyes met hers. She sat in shock and stared back at him. "And I know I may not live to see tomorrow, but I didn't want to die without telling you." Ouji's voice grew small.

Jax was so shocked, she didn't know what to say. "Ouji I..."

"I'm sorry, I-I have a lot on my mind." Ouji started to ramble.

"It's okay." She raised his chin with her nose so their eyes could meet. "I love you too, you crazy cat." She nuzzled his cheek.

The hair on Ouji's face ruffled up and the black cat turned away. "And I know I won't be able to give you kittens, but I promise to take care of you for as long as I live."

"Kittens? Slow down, tiger," Jax laughed.

"I'm serious." Ouji looked at her.

"Ouji, I don't care about all that stuff."

"But maybe later you might." Ouji sighed.

Jax chuckled and pawed him on the face. "Ouji, all that matters is that you stay the same crazy cat I met back at the old shed in the city, and that you never forget who you are and how far you've come."

Ouji smiled and nodded as he purred and rubbed against her. Especially with the stress of the day, he felt better getting his feelings out and into the open. He didn't like to keep things to himself. The two snuggled together in the cold winter air under the full moon.

Ouji woke the next morning to a snowflake on his nose. He opened his eyes and sheepishly looked around. He thought it was raining but the sky was full of falling snowflakes. It was the first snow of the winter. He stretched and looked into the gray sky and watched each snowflake as it drifted and melted on the ground where it landed. Jax woke up next to him when he moved.

"Hey it's snowing." She looked around.

"I've never been out in the snow before." Ouji flicked his tail back and forth.

"It's beautiful, but it can be a pain in the butt if you're out in it for too long," Jax warned. Ouji nodded and the two jumped around and caught snowflakes on their noses.

Senior scowled as he watched the group from afar. He had woken up before the sun rose. He stared at the group in displeasure, hating how they slowed him down, hating that they had to take so many breaks. He'd waited patiently all his life for this chance, but now it felt like time was moving slower than ever. His grandchildren walked up from behind him.

Brett sniffed the cold air. "We better move. Snow's only going to get worse."

Senior grunted and nodded. "Let's move!" the older cat yelled. "We're almost there. It'll only be a few days' walk now."

Senior led the group deeper into the forest as the snow fell. It got colder the deeper they walked into the mountains. The trees were already stripped of their leaves and stood like stone statues against the mountain's backdrop. Ouji stared up at the sky. There was very little life around, other than a lone black bird. It stared down at them from its high perch in the sky. It tilted its head, cawed, and fluttered away. It felt so empty and cold, as if life had never touched this side of the forest. Ouji looked ahead and tried to focus on getting to paradise as the snow started to fall harder. It started to stick and blanketed the forest floor in a light sheet of white. It was beautiful but painfully cold, and the group had to press on. When the snow picked up they begged Senior to stop, but they couldn't rest in the heavy snow. Puck and Missy huddled close together to guard the kittens from the falling snow. Ouji and Jax walked close behind Senior, the snow falling so hard it was impossible to see the tail of the cat in front of them. The black cat struggled to lift his paws in the three inches of snow. For the first time since starting his journey, Ouji felt like he wanted to give up. He missed his little bed downstairs in his warm home, he missed his two meals a day, and sleeping in the cozy bed next to Samantha. He wished he could just fall asleep and wake up in his bed. Ouji sighed, and didn't realize that in the midst of all his thinking he had fallen behind. He huffed and nearly collapsed in the snow. He could see the rest of the group pushing forward, their bodies turning from solid figures into shadows amongst the trees. Ouji stopped and stood alone in the snow. He groaned and asked himself why he'd ever decided to go on such a foolish journey. He was tired and cold, and things would only get worse as winter started to set in. He wasn't cut out for this; he was a house cat. He belonged in a home, with humans, not outside in this. Who was he trying to kid? An image of Jax flashed in his mind, her big green eyes staring into his as she purred. He could feel her gray and black spotted fur rubbing against his so close that he could feel her heart beat. He closed his eyes. There was no feeling like it: her purrs, her kind words. He could imagine her scent, and it ignited a flame deep inside of him. Before he knew it he was moving again, one paw in front of the other. The little black house cat from the suburbs pushed harder than he had ever had in his entire life, against the snow and the gray skies and silence of the winter forest. He kept moving, unaware that from the trees he was being watched.

When there was a break in the snow, the group desperately looked for a place to rest for the night. They had moved off course during the mid-day snow storm. Brett went out up ahead and searched for a place to rest. He found an old dead hollowed out tree. It was just big enough for the group to sleep in. Senior stood, looking around. He had no idea where they were. Everyone was dead tired and he knew that, but still he wanted to press forward. He looked back at the mother and her kittens. They would never make it. He needed to backtrack, find his way back to the river.

"Bre." He turned to his granddaughter. "We need to find our way back to the river." She nodded. "Take your brother and search through the night." He ordered.

"Yes grandfather." She did as she was told without hesitation.

Bre searched for her brother who was perched atop a fallen log. Bre stood behind him without making any noise, but she knew he'd turn around anyway.

Brett jumped down and greeted his sister.

"Grandfather wants us to backtrack to the river."

Brett sighed. "Bre, we've been hiking all morning. Don't you think we should rest?"

"We can rest when we get to paradise." Bre turned away from him.

"If we make it," Brett said under his breath.

Bre turned back. "You dare doubt grandfather?" She stepped so close to him that she was just inches from his face. "After all he has done for us."

Brett lowered his eyes. How could he forget all that Senior had done for him? However, living with Senior was no walk in the park. Their grandfather had been hard on them all their lives, training them to hunt and survive from a very young age. He guarded them ruthlessly from other cats and never let them out of his sight. Through Brett's entire life he never remembered having any friends other than Bre. Grandfather would tell them to only trust blood and stay away from the lies and tricks of the city cats.

"I do not doubt him, but I am tired, Bre. Don't you think we should take just a little rest? We've hunted and scouted for him this entire trip without question, without break."

Bre glared at her brother. "If you want to rest and take it easy, you can do so while I go out and do my job," Bre retorted.

Brett growled under his breath, but she was right. Senior had given everything to protect and raise them. "You're right. How could I be so selfish." Brett joined his sister.

Back at the hollowed out tree, everyone was fast asleep. They were hungry and tired but no one could hunt with their paws wet and fur cold. So they slept through the night without a single meal for that day and woke up the next day around noon. Senior, as always, was the first up. He walked outside to greet Bre and Brett who had been out all night tracking and who also managed to hunt them down a nice sized rabbit for them to eat.

"I trust that you have good news?" Senior took his half of the rabbit and sunk his fangs into the still warm flesh.

Bre spoke first. "Yes Grandfather. There are two paths down the river. If we stick low to the ground we can walk through the valley. It's an easy passage, but the valley walls are high and who knows what may be lurking in the shadows."

Brett stepped forward. "We also found strange droppings and skeletons of smaller animals at the foot of the valley."

Senior grunted. "And the other path?"

"It takes us high above the valley. We would have to climb to get there and walk above the river. The climb would be hard and long but we would have the advantage of sight. Nothing can hide in plain view." Bre added.

"Which is the fastest?" Senior asked without looking at them.

"They are about the same." Brett added.

Senior looked at his two grandchildren. "Which would you recommend, Bre?" He stared at Bre.

This made Brett uncomfortable. He hoped his grandfather hadn't heard him complaining the day before.

Bre smiled and took pride in her new found favoritism. "I would recommend taking the hike up above the valley."

Senior nodded. Senior took his rabbit to eat in peace and left the other rabbit to his grandchildren. "We'll leave when the sun reaches its highest point." Senior turned.

Bre nodded. "Tell the others. I'm going to guard Grandfather."

Brett nodded. He took the rabbit to the others. Brett walked into the hollow of the tree. Everyone was resting in a ball. The kittens were still sleeping between their mother.

"Here." Brett tossed the rabbit to the group. "We leave when the sun reaches its highest point," the black and gold spotted cat said as he started to turn away.

Puck got up and nearly knocked over Brett when he head-butted him in the shoulder. "Brett, what would we do without you and your sister?" He purred.

Brett gave a weak smile and slumped back into the shadows of the tree, watching everyone from afar and wondering how they could be so trusting. Puck brought this new cat into the group and everyone was practically ready to lay their lives down for him. Brett would never be so foolish to allow someone he'd just met to get that close, but something about the picture warmed him. He had never known a world outside his sister and grandfather. He remembered watching all the other kittens play when Senior would take them into town, and he always used to wish that he could join them. He got by because of his sister, so he was rarely alone, but he was always curious about the ways of the other cats in the city. Brett stretched and rested. He was grateful that his grandfather decided to leave so late; he needed his rest.

Senior sat alone atop a stump, looking through the naked trees towards the mountains. His dreams, his hopes and aspirations were so close, he could practically taste the fresh waters of paradise. This day he had been waiting for all his life, and this was the moment he'd been longing for. He turned his right ear when he heard Bre stir.

"You know what I see when I look out into the forest?"

Bre paused. She hadn't thought her grandfather had heard her.

"A whole new world ready to be conquered," Senior grunted. "All we would need are a few smart individuals and we could start a cat colony of our own." Senior turned and walked towards his granddaughter and circled around her. "I don't know if I trust the others as much as I trust you. You remind me of your mother. Everyday I see her in you, but in our perfect world you and I cannot repopulate."

"Are you suggesting...?" Bre was skeptical.

"Heavens no." Senior stepped back and chuckled. "I'm talking about the kittens."

"Missy's kittens?"

"Our kittens," Senior whispered in her ear. "She nearly killed them by not looking after them. What mother would be so careless? And the fat one, Puck, could you see him as a father? The black cat is neutered and Jax? She's strong and smart, but I think she's jealous of you."

Bre looked at her grandfather. This was a lot to take in. She had never had a reason to doubt her grandfather. He had always been right about everything: life, trusting other cats, even about Lion's Rock, but what he was suggesting now sounded like madness.

"We cannot take Missy's kittens from her." Bre had to put her paw down.

Senior glared behind her back. "Did I say take? No, I mean rescue. You were not there when she let her poor little kittens nearly drown in the river. It was terrifying. You think Puck would be a better father than me?" Senior said with venom in his voice. "And you, my dear, you would make a fine mother. This is for the better. We are the strongest, the smartest, the best prepared. You wouldn't want a bunch of buffoons raising the future of our clan, would you? You wouldn't let a bunch of outsiders dirty our blood and make us weak." Senior's voice was a whisper in her ear.

Bre stared at the group, conflicted. She didn't feel much of anything for Missy or the others, but the idea of taking kittens from their mother bothered her. On the other hand Senior was wise beyond his years and he had raised her and her brother even in his old age. When she and Brett were Missy's kittens' age, they were already hunting and tracking out with their grandfather. If they allowed Missy to continue to raise them, who knows if they would even survive?

"Have you told Brett?"

The mention of his grandson's name struck a nerve but Senior breathed in and relaxed his body and turned towards her. "I will inform him, but I need to know if you're with me or not."

Bre thought for a second, but eventually agreed. Her grandfather had never led her wrong.

"Good. Thank you my dear." Senior smiled and sent her away. Now his vision was coming full circle. All that was left was figuring out a way to get those kittens.

Chapter Nine

When the sun reached its highest point the group set off again. Senior led them through the snow. Some of it had melted over the day but not all of it. The contrast of white snow and the trees made the cold forest seem surreal. Icicles formed from the branches of the trees and dropped crystal clear droplets of water all around them. It was beautiful.

Jax walked close to Ouji, but when he was distracted she slipped away. She backed away and hid in a deep patch of snow and stalked quickly in front of him. She waited for the right moment before jumping out and pouncing on him, taking him completely off guard. The two rolled through the soft white snow together, as Puck and Missy watched from a few feet away.

"Mama, can we join?" Serma asked.

The kittens had been on lockdown after their little river stunt. Missy gave them a hard look, but then smiled bright and wide.

"Sure, but be careful!" she shouted as she watched her kittens jump on Ouji's back.

In the city they never got snow that stayed this white and pretty, and in the suburbs Ouji was never allowed to go outside and play in it. The gang played tag through the forest, making long tracks of paw prints in the snow. The kittens ran past Bre, Brett, and Senior, with Ouji and Jax in tow. The older cat glared and stole a glance to Bre, but did nothing more.

"Can't catch me! Can't catch me!" Serma yelled. He ran until he crossed another set of paw prints. "Look! There are other cats!"

The others rushed over to look. The paw prints were very similar but a little bigger than theirs and looked fresh and followed the path to the valley. Senior looked at Bre. They were not alone.

"Lets keep moving," Senior commanded.

The little ones lingered and looked at the paw prints a little longer. Serma pressed his tiny paw in the middle of the print. It was much bigger than his little paw. The little kitten smiled until his mother called for him.

"Coming!" Serma turned and ran to catch up with his mother and siblings.

Towards the end of the day just before the sun was about to set the snow picked up again. They were half way to the river, but didn't want to risk getting caught in another snow storm again.

Senior turned to Bre. "How long until we reach the river?"

"It's not far, we are very close." Bre paused and sniffed the air. It smelled like it was going to rain. She looked back at her grandfather.

Senior nodded, he could smell the rain too, and turned to the group. "We'll camp when get close to the river," he shouted as the snow turned to a freezing drizzle.

Ouji looked at Jax. He didn't think the kittens would make it that long. He thought they should get out of this freezing rain as soon as possible.

"Hey Senior," Ouji shouted from behind.

The old cat grunted. "What is it?"

"Don't you think we should call it a night?" Ouji asked as the rain picked up.

Puck nodded. "Yeah, I'm going to have to agree with Ouji here. It's starting to rain harder."

Senior's eye twitched. "We'll camp when we get to the river."

"But..." Ouji shook the rain from his fur.

Senior stopped and turned. "If you have a problem with the way I lead this group then maybe you would like to lead it instead," the old cat hissed.

All eyes were on Ouji. The group was wet and tired and the rain didn't show any signs of letting up.

"I-I just think it would be better if we stopped and rest for the night. We can pick up tomorrow," Ouji stuttered.

Senior snarled. "You challenging me boy?" The drizzle was turning into a steady pour and there was a faint rumble through the forest.

"No-no, I'm just saying." Ouji stepped back.

Senior stared him down in the rain. He was older, but his age meant he had been in more fights in his lifetime and was much more experienced in dealing with challengers.

"What! You want to lead? You want to challenge me!" He stared down the younger cat.

Lightning flashed and lit up the entire forest. The rain poured, drowning out any other sound. Ouji turned to his friends for backup but none would speak out. They wanted to stop but there was no shelter here.

"I'm, I'm sorry." Ouji stepped down.

"That's what I thought boy." Senior turned. "We camp at the river!" He shouted.

The group moved fast in the freezing rain; it was cold and unbearable but they had to keep going. Jax and Puck rubbed against Ouji for sticking up for them. They appreciated his efforts, even if they had been futile. They walked for what seemed like hours before they finally arrived at the river basin. They would have been relieved, but the path down to the river was steep and slick with mud and it would impossible to climb down. Senior insisted. They pressed on in the rain, trying to be extra cautious climbing down the slope.

Suddenly the earth started to rumble. The ground shifted and moved below them. Before they had a chance to react they were trapped in the pathway of a mudslide. The mud slid down the middle of the group, dividing them and carrying with them dirt, rocks, and trees. Senior and Bre ran frantically towards the river, but Brett was caught in the mudslide. He shouted for his sister and grandfather but they could not hear him over the sound of the rain and moving earth. Ouji and the rest of the group tried to run back up the river bank but it was nearly impossible to climb up the loose earth. Puck slipped and knocked the whole group into the quickly moving mud. The mud poured into the river, washing everyone downstream.

Senior and Bre ran as fast as they could, but a wall of earth came crashing down on them and they too were swept away. Fighting for her life, Bre swam heard towards her grandfather. He saw her and shouted to her to save the kittens. She could barely hear him but got the message and turned to where he was looking. The tiny kittens had gotten lucky this time and found a log to float on. She swam towards them and was able to grab hold of the log and guide them towards Senior with her strong legs.

Ouji was swept away from his friends by the force of the river's currents. The water was cloudy and filled with debris making it impossible for him to see let alone swim. He paddled hard but couldn't find Jax or Puck or anyone, so he swam for the shore hoping that the others would do the same.

The river was polluted with trees, grass, and dirt. It was impossible for Missy to find her kittens as she herself struggled to keep afloat. She called and called for them in the water as she swam, but it was hopeless. Puck found Missy and grabbed her by the scruff and pulled her to shore. She fought him but he knew that if they stayed in the water any longer they would both freeze.

Once Ouji made it to the shore he searched the water for his friends. He ran down the banks in hopes that they had swam to the shore. It was hard to see but as he ran he saw a body struggle to get up. He picked up the pace and helped pull the mud-covered creature from the water. When it meowed, he realized it was Jax. He helped her to the shore, relieved that she was okay. Puck, who was not far away, helped Missy to her feet, but as soon as she got up she ran down the shore to look for her kittens, searching the waters for any sign of her babies. She could not give up. Somewhere out there were her kittens and she would not lose them again.

The rapids were strong and fast but Bre and Senior helped push the kittens to shore. Senior was the first to reach the banks and helped get the kittens to safety while the rain poured around them. Bre held the log in place but the debris in the water kept knocking into her body and she could barely keep it in place. When Senior grabbed the final kitten he went back for his granddaughter.

"Grandfather!" Bre shouted in the rain as she struggled to keep her head up.

She couldn't hold on for any longer. He looked at his granddaughter, but there was another familiar rumble in the ground. There was going to be another mudslide. Senior had to choose between saving his granddaughter or getting the kittens to safety. He looked at the tiny kittens and then back at his granddaughter.

"I'm sorry dear, but some things are just more important." Senior ran towards the kittens.

Bre cried out but a log slammed into her body and swept her under the current. Senior hurried the kittens up the ravine to safety. They were scared but Senior was able to find shelter in a tiny hollowed out tree. He comforted them and kept them warm for the night.

Just a half a mile down river Ouji and Jax reunited with Puck and Missy. Puck was dragging Missy away from the river; it was hopeless now to try and search for the kittens. It was getting darker and there were no sign of them, the twins, or Senior. They climbed up the ravine and found shelter in a patch of bushes. They huddled tightly together and waited out the storm until morning.

Chapter Ten

The sun rose on a sorrow filled day. Everyone was cold and starving. No one had the strength to get up and hunt. Missy laid in the dirt lifelessly. As far as she was concerned, she had died the moment she stopped looking for her kittens. Puck stood beside her, with a heavy heart. He felt it was his fault for inviting her along, but now was not the time to lay blame and fight. Puck stood and shook the half dried mud from his fur.

"Ouji, Jax can you keep Missy warm?"

Ouji nodded and moved his aching body next to Missy's.

"Where are you going?" Jax asked.

"Back to the river bank."

Missy lifted her head, desperately wanting to join him but she didn't have the strength. She silently thanked him, holding on to the fleeting idea that her kittens were still alive. Puck used the rest of his strength to head down to the river. He searched the banks for any signs of his friends, but it was impossible to tell path from mud. The terrain looked like a can of tuna, all mashed up and mixed together. He searched up and down the river. It was hopeless but he would not give up. When he happened upon a few dead fish that had washed up on the banks, he smiled. If he could not bring back good word of his friends, he could at least bring back food.

When he reached his friends in the patch of bushes in his heart he half expected to see Senior glaring at him with the kittens running in circles around their mother. It was wishful thinking and he could hope, but the scene was the same. His friends were sad, hungry, and covered in dirt. He felt a tiny prick in his soul. He took a deep breath; another sad face wasn't going to do them any good. They needed to regroup and recover if they wanted to find the others and make it to paradise.

"Breakfast anyone?" Puck dropped the fish at their paws.

"Wow! Thanks Puck!" Ouji ran over to the pile. He carried one to Missy and one to Jax. He and Puck split the biggest one.

"No problem. We're going to need our strength." Puck tried to lighten the mood.

Jax looked around. "Still no sign of the others?"

Puck shook his head. "But hey, we'll find them. I'm sure they're okay. If I know Senior, it'll take a lot more than a little mud to take down that old bag of bones." Puck chuckled.

His positive mood was contagious. The others found comfort in his words. They rested for the day while Puck, Jax, and Ouji took turns searching the river banks. They ended their day resting together in the safety of their tiny fur ball. That night Puck couldn't sleep. He was worried about their next move. He didn't know where paradise was, but he did know that Senior insisted on following the path up the river. If they'd got separated he was sure Senior and the rest of the group would head there. Puck looked up at the night sky, perfectly clear under the crescent moon. He watched the stars shine and then saw one shoot across the sky. The old cat's tale says that if you wished upon a shooting star your wish would surely come true and right now the only thing the orange tabby wanted was his friends to be safe and sound. He smiled at his wishful thinking, but it helped him get to sleep.

The following morning Puck woke up early to check the river bank for more fish. It was hard work and there was barely enough for a one cat to eat, but he managed to find four small fish. He brought them back to his friends, who were very happy indeed.

"I'm in no rush, but if I were Senior I would be heading up river." Puck dropped a fish at each of his friend's paws. "I figure he'll send Bre and Brett after us and they're the best trackers in the world, but with all that mud and water it might be hard to sniff us out. That's why I think we should continue on. That's what Senior would do."

"But we don't know where paradise is," Jax said sadly.

Puck sighed. "But we do know how to get there." Puck turned and faced the river. "Paradise is located at the mouth of the river. If we keep going upriver we should get there or at least run into the others." Puck turned to his friends, but they didn't seem convinced. "Come on guys, we need to make a scent. Bre and Brett can't track us if we don't move."

Ouji and Jax looked at each other, then back at Puck.

"We need to leave a trail, something to find us by." Puck scratched at the dirt and rubbed his butt on the ground.

Jax gave him a weird look. "Okay okay, I get it." She turned to the others. "If we start to make tracks I'm sure the twins can pick it up."

Ouji nodded. "Missy?"

Missy half smiled. "I'll be okay."

Puck nodded. "We'll leave in a few hours."

"Good." Ouji yawned. "Because I could use a bath and a nap."

"I'm with you." Jax looked at all the caked on dirt on her fur.

Puck smiled and watched his friends leave to go down to the river. He turned to Missy who looked half awake.

"Missy, are you thirsty?" He stood over her.

She shook her head.

"Come on Missy." He nudged her with his cheeks. "You have to eat and drink to keep your strength up."

Missy sighed, but he was right. She didn't want to admit that she didn't have the strength to carry on. She tried to stand but her legs were weak from exhaustion. She stood and wobbled over, but Puck was quick to catch her, supporting her with his weight.

"Thank you Puck." She smiled.

"No problem my dear. All aboard the river water express?" He pointed.

"Why yes please mister conductor, but I don't have my ticket." She faked a frown.

"That's okay, pretty ladies ride for free." He chuckled and winked before nuzzling her cheek.

She laughed honestly for the first time since the storm. Puck was good like that, always able to draw up a smile. Puck slid under her and carried her to the river bank. She was very grateful. The water was so much clearer now that all the mud had washed away. It was still very cold but refreshing and crisp. The two bathed and relaxed on the riverside and watched the water glisten.

"Missy, I just wanted to say-"

"Don't. I was the one who agreed to come along." She stared sadly into the unforgiving waters.

"But if I hadn't invited you…"

"I would be back in that stuffy old city and not out here enjoying the fresh forest air." She turned to him, and she couldn't blame him. He had only wanted to give her a better life for her and her kittens.

Puck turned. "Missy."

She looked at him and laid her head on the folds of his neck. She purred the sound so strong that he felt it in his bones.

"Missy." He closed his eyes and purred in response. What was done was done. If she was okay with moving on, so was he. He would get them to paradise if it was the last thing he would do.

Brett awoke the next morning in a puddle of mud and dirt. His thin body was half submerged in the river and the other half was laying on the shallow river bank. He stared at the ground in a fog. He had not yet come to terms at what he'd seen and heard from the night before. He closed his eyes but couldn't get his mind to focus on anything other than Senior turning his back on his sister. He couldn't hear what they were saying, but the look on Senior's face as he let her get washed away turned his stomach upside down. Brett opened his eyes. He felt a shiver run up his spine as it finally registered that he was still half submerged in cold water. He dragged himself onto the river bank with his front paws and collapsed in the wet dirt. A falcon circled above. He would be dead meat if he stayed here. He needed to move. He lifted himself onto all fours and hurried best he could for cover into a thick leafy snow covered bush. He collapsed in the dirt, positive his eyes were lying to him. His grandfather would never abandon his sister. He loved her. He and Bre were his only family. He tried to convince himself, but the images flashing before his eyes were making it harder and harder to believe it hadn't happened. When he finally was able to fall asleep, he dreamed of him and his sister.

Two tiny eight-month-old kittens ran down the streets of the city, hot on the tail of their first street rat under the watchful eyes of their grandfather. They cornered the rat in an alley, fangs and teeth bared as the rodent hissed at them. They charged, stepping over each other's paws as the rat slipped away. They were acting as individuals and not a team. They slammed into each other again as their grandfather glared at them, giving them disapproving looks. They would not win alone and they realized that. The twins quickly exchanged looks and attacked together as one. They trapped the rat behind a trash can, with one chasing it into the mouth of the other. The deed was done. They caught the rat as a team and their grandfather was so proud. Little Brett looked up as his dream turned dark.

"Grandfather!" Bre screamed only moments before the log swept her underwater.

"Bre!" Brett woke up screaming in the cold of the night. He was panting and crying, blowing out large puffs of white air into the darkness. "Bre!" he shouted. For the first time in his life, he realized that he was truly alone.

Chapter Eleven

Puck lead the group up river, all in better spirits after a good night's sleep and a solid meal before their hike. They maintained hope that they would soon be reunited with Senior and the rest of the group and Puck did his best to keep everyone motivated. He joked and laughed and carried on with his usual jolly demeanor and soon he had everyone joking and laughing right along with him. They reached a fork in the road that split into two paths, one through the valley and one over the valley. Not sure which path to take Puck decided to check each one, he ran a few yards up to see which one was better and reported back to his friends.

"Looks like we have two options." He led his friends a little ways up the rocky cliff. "We can walk up and around." He indicated the exit of the valley that was many yards away over rocky dry terrain. "Or we can go through the valley. Both routes lead to the river."

"The walk up these hills seem awfully steep," Missy pointed out.

Jax looked up the mountainous path. It was covered with rocks and was very uneven. "I agree, it would be too dangerous to cross up here. We should take the valley."

"Good idea. A fall from here could be a real neck breaker." Puck added. "Okay! Onward!" He led his friends down the cliff and into the narrow valley.

Gold eyes watched from the cliffs above as the group moved through the narrow passage way. The path was barely wide enough for them to walk side by side, but the group was in no hurry. They were more concerned with leaving a trail for their friends to follow than pondering the safety of the valley they were walking through. Quick feet moved above them, so quiet that not a pebble of dirt stirred. They'd been tracking the group ever since they neared the mountains and never would have expected them to walk right into their little trap without coaxing. Soon the pack was gathered and waiting at, the widest part of the valley. They stood nine strong and eager, waiting for Puck and his friends to arrive.

Neither Puck nor the others could see that Puck was leading his friends into a trap, and there was little anyone could do about it. They joked and laughed and listened to his stories without a care in the world. The group walked around the bend, where they reached a part of the valley that was much wider and more spacious than the rest. It was eerily quiet. Puck and Ouji continued to laugh, but Jax sensed something was not right. She looked around and noticed little piles of bones scattered in the shadows of the walls of the valley. She looked up and thought she saw shadows in the sunlight. Before she could call out a warning, a group of wildcats attacked the group. These cats were much larger than the ones back home, with their gold eyes and sandy brown striped fur and bobbed tails setting them apart. They cornered the group, staring them down with fearsome intensity. Puck and the gang huddled close together as the wildcats circled and hissed, exposing their sharp fangs.

"What--what kind of cats are these?" Ouji whispered into Puck's ear.

"Your guess is as good as mine." Puck stole glances between each of the four cats surrounding them.

"You're a long way from home, house cats," one of the wildcats growled their voice low.

The group could barely make out what they were saying. The wildcats had an accent they'd never heard before, as if they were from a different world. The other wildcats growled and snickered.

"Now, let us not hurry. Take your time, brothers and sisters," the first cat spoke again.

The four approached as the sounds of laughter circled through the valley. More wildcats flooded in, blocking their way back. They were trapped and there was only one way out.

Puck nudged Ouji and whispered in his ear. "We need to make a run for it." Ouji agreed but the wildcats had them boxed in, there was no way out.

The wildcats laughed and toyed with them, but the group wasn't ready to give up. They made a split second decision to run and took off, Ouji and Puck pushing their way past two of the giant brown cats. The two remaining cats chased after them. As they ran they could hear chants and cheers coming from the walls, where other faces were starting to appear. Everyone ran as hard as they could, but Missy was the slowest and didn't stand a chance as one of the wildcats jumped and knocked her to the ground. She screamed and the rest of the group stopped. Puck growled and turned back as fast as he could and ran right for Missy. The wildcat who had tackled her gladly ran past her to accept the foolish city cat's challenge. They slammed into each other and tussled in the dirt. The remaining wildcats ran straight for Ouji and Jax. Ouji saw where they were headed and ran in the other direction. He hoped that two of the three would follow him so that Jax had a chance to escape, but Ouji wasn't as fast as Jax. She was able to keep on her toes and steer clear of the wildcats' claws. Ouji ran but was easily cornered by two of the wil cats.

"Nowhere to run, house cat," the female wildcat said, her voice husky.

Ouji growled and instead of running away he charged right for her. He knew that he could not outrun them but if he could somehow slow them down maybe it would give his friends enough time to run away. Their body wasn't much different from his but what they lacked in size they made up for in experience. The wildcat knocked Ouji to the group. They were fast and strong from years of hunting and surviving out in the forest and it showed. Ouji didn't have time to dwell on experience versus inexperience before the wildcats were on him again. They scratched and bit him and flung him around like a toy. They laughed and pounced on him until he could no longer walk. Ouji was nearly done for when he saw an opening and lunged for one of the wildcat's necks. With his last ounce of strength, he bit down and didn't let go. The wildcat screamed and kicked and rolled in the dirt furiously, but Ouji held tight. The other wildcats bit and pulled at Ouji's tail until he finally let go. He fell on top of the wildcat that was biting his tail and landed on his head. They rolled but the wildcat was quick on his feet.

"That's enough!" shouted someone from high above.

The wildcats froze and stepped away. When the dust cleared Ouji could tell that his friends had taken quite the beating. Puck and Missy were wounded and laying in the dirt beside one another and Jax was standing but breathing heavily next to them. Ouji turned and watched as the pack of wildcats parted to let their leader through. She was the tallest of the pack and had a spotted coat with piercing hazel eyes. She held her short bobbed tail high in the air, that had a black tip the same color as the points on her ears. She stopped some feet away from Ouji with a grin on her face. She sat calmly in the dirt across from him.

"House cat, you and your friends have entertained me enough for the day. So I shall make a deal with you." Her grin widened. "Leave the fat one and the weak one behind and I'll let you leave with your little girlfriend or..." Her eyes glinted with humor. "Stay and fight my strongest warrior and die. It's your choice, house cat."

Ouji turned and looked at Puck and Missy. There was no way he was going to abandon them, but then he looked at Jax. A deal would save them both, but his heart would not let him live knowing that some of his friends would die. He turned and looked at Puck.

The orange tabby was tired. They made eye contact and the fat cat nodded as if to forgive Ouji if he made the latter choice. Missy closed her eyes. She thought only of her kittens and how soon she would be reunited with them in the afterlife. They were both willing to die to let Ouji and Jax go free. Ouji dug his claws into the dirt. He didn't make it all this way to bail on his friends. If he couldn't make it to paradise, at least they would. He looked around him. He had no way of knowing if she would let them go free or send her pack after them, but this was the only chance he would have to save them all.

"I accept your challenge!" Ouji shouted bravely.

"Ouji no!" Jax interjected, but two bobcats stepped in front of her.

The leader grinned. "I'm not sure what selfless victory you're trying to claim, but I will be entertained nevertheless," the bobcat queen shouted. "Let them go!"

Puck and the others shook their heads. He and the others weren't going to leave without their friend.

The bobcat queen glared at them. "Go or die here with your foolish friend; the choice is yours. It matters little to me." She growled.

Puck stood his ground. He was ready to fight and so were Jax and Missy. They weren't going to leave Ouji behind; they were in this together.

"Ouji!" Jax stepped forward, ready to fight.

"Go!" Ouji shouted. He kept his eyes from his friends and stared only at the bobcat queen.

"But Ouji!" Jax shouted.

"Get out of here!" He did not turn and face them. This was the only chance they had to make it out alive and Ouji was ready to lay down his life for his friends. He prayed they'd leave and take the chance he'd given them, for he feared the bobcat's patience would not last long.

Puck frowned, but he did not want to disrespect Ouji's choice. He was doing this for them. "Come on," Puck said.

Missy and Jax lingered for a second before they were pushed out by the growls of the bobcats. Ouji watched his friends with worry as the bobcats chased them out.

"Fear not, house cat. I am a feline of my word." She grunted loudly and called back her bobcats.

Now Ouji was left alone with the pack of growling bobcats. They all grinned, circling around him. The queen chuckled and yowled lifting a paw into the air. From her side a tall muscular bobcat appeared before him. She was as big as the queen with thin black stripes around her paws and large white rings around her golden eyes.

"This is Balbina. She is the covenant's strongest feline. Do not bother with your chauvinistic chivalry, she will not go easy on you as she expects the same. Winner is the last feline standing and the prize is walking away with your life." The queen bobcat yowled into the air, loud enough that it could be heard throughout the entire valley.

Puck turned when he heard. "Good luck kid." He continued to run through the valley where the group was prepared to wait for Ouji's return.

Ouji and Balbina stood alone in the circle of bobcats. They were cheering and roaring much like when Ouji helped Puck and Ellie take down Koga, but this time it was Ouji standing alone. His heart pounded in his chest as he circled around the larger cat. She could see through his black fur and thick frame. She could tell Ouji was not a fighter, and Ouji knew it, but his fight would not be in vain. He thought of Jax and the rest of his friends. He prayed they would make it to paradise, that Missy would be reunited with her kittens, and for

Senior and the twins to be okay. He silenced his mind and focused. He closed his eyes and exhaled.

Balbina roared and lunged. Ouji was quick on his feet and dodged. She chased him around the circle as the others cheered. He stopped and slid in the dirt before sinking his claws deep into the rocky soil and lunging back at her. She took the blow with little reaction the way she held her weight making it impossible to knock her over. Instead, the move had left him open. She lunged at his shoulder and bit him. He hissed and swatted at her ear. She pulled back and grinned as she ran to the other side of the circle. When their eyes met they charged, but this time he leaped with his claws at the last moment, bearing his teeth and claws locking her in a hold, but she was able to break the claw hold and get at his under belly. Ouji yelped when he felt her long claws scratch his stomach. He jumped back and rolled into the dirt.

The crowd cheered. Balbina walked happily around beaming with pride and envy from the crowd. Ouji panted heavily. He looked at the queen, who was grinning and staring down at him. He closed his eyes. If he gave up now, he would no longer have to suffer. Ouji looked up at Balbina, and she smirked.

"It looks as though you will have another trophy Balbina!" the queen shouted. "Now finish him!"

Balbina nodded and readied herself to make the final attack. Ouji gazed up. It was like everything around him was moving in slow motion. The roars of the bobcats around him faded out. He could no longer focus on Balbina charging towards him, all he could think of was gray and black fur and two big green eyes staring at him. He closed his eyes and as the image cleared, a small triangle shaped face appeared. He stared into its eyes and every memory of Jax and his entire life flashed before him until it all faded out and all that was left was the sound of his mother quietly humming to him. Was this truly the end? Would he ever understand why he was here and what the meaning of his seemingly short existence was? A flame awakened deep inside of him, an untapped force that surged through his veins. His heart jumped into overdrive. He didn't want to die here, not after all that he had been through.

He opened his eyes right as Balbina was right above of him, high in the air with her claws bare. Ouji did not run, but instead lunged into her, taking the full force of her claws. She scratched him hard down his left eye. He felt the blood drip down his face, the adrenaline pumping through his veins and muting the pain. He recovered and stood in the damp earth, panting. All the bobcats watched in surprise. Silence hovered over the group, but when Ouji readied himself for another blow they crowd watched in amazement. Balbina roared. She was not afraid and welcomed the fight, happy to deliver his death nice and slow if that was what he preferred. She charged, aiming for his neck this time. Ouji moved out of the way just in time, but snapped around to sink his teeth into the side of her neck. She wailed and the two rolled in the dirt, drawing up clumps of dirt and rocks as they threw each other around. Ouji was determined to win this. He was prepared to give it his all, or die trying.

Balbina managed to kick him off. She didn't expect the tiny house cat to make such a powerful comeback, but still she was not afraid. She was a warrior and warriors did not feel fear. She rolled over and charged at him again, but Ouji was too quick. He ducked under her and bit her back leg. She growled and hissed as she fell to the ground. She knocked Ouji off but she was wounded. Her fellow bobcats were shocked but dared not interfere. Balbina prepared herself. She guarded her weakness by focusing on her other paws. Ouji turned and faced her.

"It doesn't have to end like this." He breathed heavily, tired.

Balbina growled. "We fight to the death!" With that, she leaped at him.

Ouji could not dodge this one and she pounced right onto his chest. Her fangs were just inches from his throat, and she snapped and bit at him but he was able to ward her off. He rolled and in turn lunged for her. She couldn't dodge in time, and as Ouji was about to deliver the final blow, a large figure eclipsed the sun. The queen looked up.

"Wolves!" she shouted.

Her fellow pack members shrunk away in fear and headed towards the entrance of the valley. The wolves leaped down from the cliffs landing all around Ouji. The little black cat collapsed in the dirt. He could not move, but at least the bobcats had ran in the opposite direction from where his friends had gone. A giant gray and black wolf approached and stood before him. Ouji looked up and into his eyes, they were as glistening as a star-filled night, peaceful and calm.

"Ouji." The wolf spoke to him in a calm and deep voice, jarring him awake. "My name is Chief and my pack has lived in these forest for hundreds of years, carefully guarding it, and protecting it from the threat of man. I have seen many creatures enter these woods. Many with strong minds and strong bodies ten times the size of yours, but none who have possessed the courage and bravery you have shown here today. You have amazed even me and for that I will share with you this: always follow your heart Ouji, even if the path takes you into the valley of darkness. Your courage will always be the light that will show you the way."

Chief gazed down at the wounded cat. His survival depended entirely on him, but the old wolf believed the little cat had more fight in him than he could ever imagine. Chief turned and the pack opened up a path for him to walk through. Ouji watched them leave, too weak to even mutter a goodbye. It was a great honor to meet the guardians of the forest. Just as Adrian said, they were the ones who watched over the forest. Ouji winced as he tried to smile. He'd done his job, he protected his friends and made it to the forest against all odds, which was more than the little house cat from the neighborhoods could have ever hoped to ask for. He gazed at the valley exit, his vision fading, and shut his eyes.

Chapter Twelve

"Ouji!" A familiar voice shouted his name. "Ouji! Ouji wake up!" The voice trembled.

Ouji slowly opened his eyes. He looked up and saw Jax standing above him.

"Ouji!" She licked his face and purred, her expression a mix of happiness and relief.

He blinked. "Jax?"

She smiled. "Ouji I'm so glad you're okay."

The two rubbed their head's against each other. He thought he would never see her again. Puck and Missy ran over too. Ouji was so happy to see his friends, but they didn't want the bobcats to corner them again so they high tailed it out of there. Ouji took one look back. It wasn't a dream, he was really visited by the guardians of the forest. Ouji smiled as he ran next to his friends, next stop paradise.

The kittens ran next to Senior as the older cat dragged his feet from behind. They had made it over the valley, but the journey had not been easy. The kittens had much more energy than he had and they had made it a game to jump on the steep rocks of the valley cliffs. Senior told the kittens that everyone had died in the mudslide. They were sad but Senior promised to take care of them, so they had continued their journey to paradise together. It started to snow again as the kittens played, catching snowflakes with their tongues and noses.

"Look Uncle Senior!" Serma shouted. "I can catch one on my nose!"

Senior grunted. He was too old to be raising kittens. "Settle down and keep moving. We don't have time to fool around." He growled.

Serma frowned and walked next to his brother and sister. He wished his mother was here. They all missed her very much and still had hope that she was out there somewhere, but as the days dragged on they began to realize that they may never see her again. Senior pressed on without resting until he reached a rocky slope. The smell was different; it was fresher here, and he could hear the sound of falling water. His eyes lit up with excitement as he rushed up the slope, leaving the kittens behind to climb for themselves. He reached the top and could have fainted. There it was: Ohajidi, paradise.

Hidden deep within the mountains of the forest was a place like no other. Waters fell from the canopy, pooling so clear he could practically see the fish swimming below. Vegetation grew wild from the mineral rich waters on the stone and around the basin of the waterfalls. It created the perfect cover from elements and their enemies. It was a sight to see and the old cat choked up with emotion. Finally after all these years, he was here. He was really here and it was all his for the taking. Senior laughed to himself when he finally remembered the kittens.

"Kittens!" He turned. "Kittens!" He froze when he saw Brett standing at the base of the slope, with the kittens hiding behind him. "Brett?" Senior coughed. "It-it's a surprise to see you. I mean," Senior walked down the slope. "I'm so glad to see you my son."

Brett ignored his grandfather's words. "Go hide," he instructed the kittens.

"But why?" Serma asked.

"Hide and don't come out until I tell you to!" Brett bared his teeth.

Senior watched the kittens scurry and hide in the bushes behind some rocks. He glared at his grandson.

"What is the meaning of this?"

Brett stared his grandfather down for the first time in his life. "Don't play dumb with me!"

Senior growled. "Don't take that tone with me! I am your grandfather. Without me you'd be dead in an alleyway."

"And Bre?" Brett stepped forward. "What of my sister? Why is she not standing here with us, right now this very second? Had you not betrayed her, she would be!"

Senior bit his tongue; he did not think his grandson had seen.

Brett huffed. He felt betrayed, angry that his grandfather let his sister perish.

Senior shook his head. "It was an accident, I swear."

"Lies!" Brett shouted.

"Look!" Senior pointed in the direction of the kittens. "I could not have saved them both!"

"I saw you turn your back on her!"

"Your eyes lie! I would never turn my back on my family; you're all I have left. I swear to you." Senior walked closer to his grandson. "I would never betray you."

Brett turned his back on his grandfather. "I-I'm..." Brett was confused. Had his eyes lied to him?

Serma snuck away when he heard the older cats shout. Uma and Tama tried to pull him back but he slipped by anyway. Serma peeked from behind the rock and saw Senior ready to leap onto Brett's back.

"Brett, behind you!" Serma shouted.

Brett turned around in just enough time to dodge his grandfather's attack. The older cat rolled and slid off the edge of the cliff. His front claws caught onto a row of protruding roots.

"Help!" Senior shouted from over the edge of the cliff. Brett ran to his grandfather. "Brett! Help!" Senior shouted.

"Only if you admit that you let Bre die! Only then will I allow you to live."

"Cut out that foolishness and help me up!" Senior growled.

Now Brett saw Senior's true colors. He didn't care about him or his sister. All he cared about was getting to paradise. Brett hissed.

"Brett! What are you waiting for? I order you to help me!" Senior shouted.

Brett looked down at his grandfather. "Help yourself." He turned his back for the last time on his grandfather.

Senior shouted and hissed as he tried to lift himself. He was so close to paradise he could smell the fresh waters of its falls. He managed to pull himself up when the root came lose and he lost his grip and fell into the rocky ravine below.

Brett turned and watched the spot where his grandfather once stood. He had no more family left. He was alone now. The kittens appeared from the bushes, scared and confused. He turned to them and smiled. Maybe family was more than blood. Maybe a true family was a group of individuals you could trust, a group of friends that had your back and loved you no matter what. He smiled softly at the kittens.

"Hey, come with me." He led them up the rocky slope to the falls basin. The kittens followed and froze in their tracks, and gazing over the ledge at the crystal clear falls below them. Never had they seen water so clear: a paradise in a dry winter forest.

"Wow!" Serma shouted as his fur warmed from the springs below.

"Whoa." Uma looked at Tama, who smiled and watched the fish below.

"Welcome to your new home, little buddies." Brett smiled as he stared at the hidden paradise below.

"I wish mama could see this." Tama's voice choked up.

Suddenly, Brett remembered that he had heard the screams of other cats back over the valley. He was so focused on tracking Senior that he didn't have any time to search for the others. He hoped it wasn't too late.

Ouji looked weird and Puck never missed an opportunity to let him know it. The orange tabby said he looked like crazy old Senior with the scar above his eye. Ouji just brushed it off, even laughing with him sometimes. Ouji was just happy to be alive, happy he was given this second chance to complete the journey with his friends.

"What are you thinking about, crazy cat?" Jax smiled and flicked her tail back and forth as she walked.

"You," Ouji retorted.

She burst into laughter. "You are so corny." She turned and head-butted him in the shoulder.

He laughed and purred as he rubbed his body on hers.

"Alright you two." Puck teased. "Get a den."

"What?" Ouji joked.

Missy smiled.

Puck looked at her and smiled back.

The bushes stirred and the group froze. Puck and Ouji were immediately on guard. They readied themselves for another encounter with the bobcats, claws and teeth ready. Then a familiar cat stepped out from the bushes.

"Brett?" Puck relaxed.

"Puck?" Brett looked around. "Missy! Ouji! Jax!"

"Brett!" They all shouted and ran and purred and rubbed against each other.

"Ow ow ow." Ouji yowled.

"Oh sorry." Jax got off of him.

Brett noticed Ouji's scar over his left eye but didn't ask. He was too excited that he had finally found them.

"I tracked you all night and all day from the valley."

"The valley?" Puck looked back.

"Don't worry, no one followed me." Brett smiled. "After all, I am the best tracker in all the lands," he boasted.

Puck laughed. "Right you are!"

"Where's Bre?" Jax asked.

Brett lowered his head. "She... She didn't make it."

Jax frowned. "I'm so sorry."

"And Senior?" Ouji asked.

Brett grunted as he tried to push any thoughts of Senior out of his mind. "I'll explain on the way. Come on!"

"On the way?" Missy looked at Puck.

Brett nodded. "I found it! I found paradise!"

The group's faces lit up with excitement.

"Then what are we standing around here for!" Puck exclaimed.

Brett took off with the group in tow. He explained everything that had happened with Bre and Senior, but best of all, he could tell Missy that not only were all three of her kittens alive and well, they were all safe in paradise at this very moment. Her face lit up and she encouraged the group to run through the night, which no one complained about. They ran until they reached the slope leading into to paradise. When they got there Brett stepped out of the way to let Missy through. She meowed and called for her kittens. She paid no mind to the scenery around her when she heard them meow back.

"Kittens!" she shouted.

"Mama!!" All three of the kittens called back and ran around the water basin to their mother.

"My babies!" She purred and groomed her kittens. "My precious babies." She was overwhelmed.

Puck was ready to choke up himself, but coughed instead, trying to hide it from his friends.

Ouji and Jax stood next to each other and smiled. They had finally made it to paradise and it was more beautiful than they could have ever imagined. Behind the crystal clear falls was a hidden cave with tiny warm blue pools that were heated by the dormant volcano below. There were plenty of fish flowing through the stream into the deep blue basin in the middle of their little paradise and above the falls was the mouth of the river that seemed to run for miles from the mountains. It was a place beyond Ouji and the others' wildest dreams, somewhere he thought he would never reach. He was grateful that he was able to find such a beautiful place and make it here with all of his friends.

Ouji turned and exited the cave to look at the stars in the cold winter sky. His ears twitched as he picked up sounds from the bushes.

"Ouji?" Adrian poked his head from the plant.

"Adrian!" Ouji got up. "Boy, am I glad to see you!" Ouji ran over to his friend and hugged him.

"It is good to see you as well, my friend." The tiny deer mouse smiled. "I'm glad you made it, it was quite hard to find this place indeed."

"Thank you." Ouji purred. "And boy do I have a story to tell you."

Adrian twitched his whiskers and settled in, just like old times.

Chapter Thirteen

Spring arrived, bringing life back to the forest. The trees bloomed and the earth, once covered in snow, was blanketed in miles of soft grass. Streams flowed over melting lumps of ice and the sky was filled with birds returning to nest. The forest was alive once more and the cats emerged to see the wonders of springtime for the first time. Over the winter Missy's kittens had grown a lot and she couldn't have been prouder. They had trained all winter long under the watchful eye of Brett and were well on their way to becoming capable hunters. Ouji also enjoyed the onset of spring. Over the winter it was decided unanimously that Ouji should lead their group and although he still had a lot to learn, with the support of his friends he felt he could do anything.

"Alright group," Ouji appeared and stood before his friends. "Shall we go out for a hunt?"

Jax hopped onto a rock near the cave wall. "Do you even have to ask?"

Ouji chuckled and turned to the rest of his friends, who were resting easy near the falls. Ouji had learned a great deal about the balance of the forest. It was a powerful, but delicate force, one governed by rules that all creatures must abide. These warnings, he took from Adrian, he heeded this time after seeing firsthand the full power of the forest. He would act more cautiously from now on and listen to his heart as well as his friends. Ouji was ready to leave with Jax when Uma appeared from behind the waterfalls, now two times the size she was before winter.

"Let us handle this Ouji." Her brothers and Brett appeared behind her.

Puck yawned. "Yeah, let the youngin's handle this one." The orange tabby settled in next to Missy.

Ouji nodded, much to the kitten's delight. He watched them take off, before his eyes wondered over to Jax. His fur puffed up when he realized she was staring right back at him. She giggled, as she trotted into the sunlight making her gray and black fur glisten in the light. She glanced at him from out the corner of her eye. Ouji's shrunk as he melted into the rocks, he still got flustered when she looked at him, but it was a feeling that he enjoyed, it meant that his love was only growing stronger. He followed her up the cliffs of their paradise home, where she paused to take in the fresh spring air.

"This is amazing right?" Ouji rubbed his head against her shoulder.

She nuzzled him back. "I could not have wished for a better ending."

"A beginning." Ouji looked her in the eyes and she lightly smiled.

The breeze picked up and Jax enjoyed one last breath before taking off into the forest. Ouji should have known, sappy moments weren't Jax's thing. He took off after her and the two ran through the woodland pasture stirring insects and flowers as they ran. They danced between each other until they reached the roaring river and followed it cliff side all the way down to the water's edge. Jax drew back taking Ouji by surprise. She stopped then pounced on his back causing the two of them to topple down to the sandy bank. Jax landed on top, laughing and caring on. Ouji laughed back, getting lost in her beautiful eyes, when suddenly they heard a branch snap. The two cats looked at the rumbling brushes and jumped to their feet when the sound grew louder. The bushes rustled and parted slowly a large familiar figure emerged.

"Kaji?" Ouji relaxed as his fur settled.

"In the flesh." Kaji said with a toothy grin. From behind him Ouji and Jax could hear the faint sounds of kittens. They both looked at each other, before turning to Kaji with puzzled looks. "Thought you two love birds could use some company." Kaji stepped back into the bushes and pulled out a large wicker basket from the brush.

Jax and Ouji sniffed the air, approaching the basket cautiously, as the sound of kittens got louder. Kaji smiled and used his nose to lift the top covering the basket. The two cats walked forward and were surprised to see five tiny two-week old kittens.

"Oh my goodness." Jax gasped as her eyes widened. "Ouji." She turned to him. Ouji couldn't believe it himself.

"Someone dumped these fellas off on the edge of town and I thought you guys could use company. After all you're gonna need a heck of a lot more of you if you're gonna to settle here." Their reaction gave Kaji the desired effect; he had done his good deed for the year.

"Ouji, do you think?" Jax glanced between Ouji and the kittens.

"I mean...if," Ouji looked back at Jax. This was sudden, but Ouji wanted nothing more but to raise kittens with Jax. The two stared at each other, as if they could read each other's mind.

"Well, what do you say?" Kaji asked impatiently.

The two cats looked at their canine friend. "Yes!"

Kaji wagged his tail and happily toted the kittens back to their paradise home. All were happy to hear about the new arrivals. Their clan would be even stronger now. In the days that followed word was sent out to Adrian and all gathered to feast and welcome the new kittens. Kaji couldn't stay long but he sent all of them his blessing. He promised to visit once every once in a while, but Ouji was just grateful to see him again and wished him luck.

Just over the cliffs, deep in the mountains. The wolves watched the cats below. Very few cats made it to paradise and it pleased Chief to see their journey come to a happy end. Chief felt it was time too, for his journey on Earth to end. He had lived for many decades and seen and met many creatures. He had lived a wonderful life, but it was time now and he was ready.

"I'm heading out father." Kaji called to his father in passing.

Chief opened his eyes and gazed into the night sky. "Kaji." Kaji froze, tense in the cool night air. He knew what was coming. He could feel it in the air. "It's time." Chief gazed over the cliff side. "I know you wish to live with the humans and I will not force you, but Kaji..." Chief paused as a light breeze blow through his aged fur. "Look over the forest, protect the creatures that reside here." Chief stared at the cheerful cats in paradise. "They are our future."

Kaji lightly grinned, before walking away. "Whatever you say old man." With that Kaji took off into the night.

Ouji looked to the mountains, listening to the howls of the wolves. He closed his eyes, silently thanking them once more for their protection. He took one last look at the moon before entering the cave to be with his friends. Lit by the moonlight from the cracks in the cave, Ouji could see the smiles and happy faces of all his friends. His best friend Adrian had arrived and with lots of goodies from his family. Brett and his apprentices had caught a mighty feast, with plenty to go around. It was more than he could have asked for. Ouji smiled as Puck ran up from behind and head-butted him in the rear.

"Now you're starting to act like an old man!" The orange tabby joked. Ouji pushed him away and flicked his tail playfully back and forth. "Hey, I'm just being honest, Mr. Father. Now are you going to keep standing here like a rock or join us?"

Ouji smiled and followed Puck to the center where everyone had gathered. "Okay, little ones." Adrian smiled. "How would you like to hear a story about the bravest cat in all the forest?" Everyone gathered round and purred as the little kittens settled next to Jax, eyes wide open staring at Adrian. He smiled and groomed his crooked whiskers with his tiny paws. "It all started in a place called a neighborhood..."

Photo Credit - Brittany Rose Photography

Blair Cousins is an aspiring writer, daydreamer, and social bumblebee. In her free time, she enjoys pursuing the great American pass time of sleeping. During her waking hours, she grinds hard to make her dreams come true.